# Love
## FROM AFAR

LOVE LETTERS FROM ELLIS CREEK
———— BOOK 1 ————

# PENNY ZELLER

Love from Afar
Copyright ©2021 by Penny Zeller
www.pennyzeller.com
All rights reserved
Published by Maplebrook Publishing

No part of this publication may be reproduced, distributed, or transmitted in any form or by any means, including photocopying, recording, or other electronic or mechanical methods, or by any information storage and retrieval system without the prior written permission of the publisher, except in the case of very brief quotations embodied in critical reviews and certain other noncommercial uses permitted by copyright law.

Cover design by Mountain Peak Edits & Design
Cover Model by Period Images and Pi Creative Lab

This novel is a work of fiction. Unless otherwise indicated, all the names, characters, businesses, places, events and incidents in this book are either a figment of the author's imagination or used in a fictitious manner. Any resemblance to actual persons, living or dead, incidents, locales, settings, organizations, businesses, or actual events is purely coincidental. Any brand names or trademarks mentioned throughout are owned by the respective companies.

All scripture quotations are taken from the King James Version of the Bible.

This novella originally appeared as part of The Secret Admirer Romance Collection. ©2017

ISBN: 978-0976083665

## ALSO BY PENNY ZELLER

**Maplebrook Publishing**

**Standalone Books**
Love in the Headlines
Freedom's Flight
Levi's Vow
Heart of Courage

**Wyoming Sunrise Series**
Love's New Beginnings
Forgotten Memories
Dreams of the Heart
When Love Comes
Love's Promise

**Horizon Series**
Over the Horizon
Dreams on the Horizon
Beyond the Horizon

**Hollow Creek Series**
Love in Disguise
Love in Store

**Love Letters from Ellis Creek Series**
Love from Afar
Love Unforeseen
Love Most Certain

**Love in Chokecherry Heights Series**
Henry and Evaline (Prequel)
Love Under Construction

**Whitaker House Publishing**

**Montana Skies Series**
McKenzie
Kaydie
Hailee

*Barbour Publishing*
Love from Afar
(The Secret Admirer Romance
Collection)

Freedom's Flight
(The Underground Railroad Brides
Collection)

**Beacon Hill Press (Nonfiction)**
77 Ways Your Family Can Make a
Difference

To my oldest daughter.
I am beyond blessed to be your mom.

*Wait on the Lord: be of good courage, and he shall strengthen thine heart; wait, I say, on the LORD.*
- Psalm 27:14

# Chapter One

ANOTHER WEDDING DRESS COMPLETED.

Another happy ending.

Just never her own.

Pushing reality aside, Meredith Waller bustled up the front steps of the Goff residence. She draped the wedding dress over her arm and tapped on the door, eager for the recipient to see her latest sewing creation.

"What a pleasure to see you. Do come in, Meredith." Mrs. Goff, a round and jolly sort, beckoned Meredith to enter the humble home she had visited so many times throughout the years.

But this time was different. This time, Meredith would be assisting her best friend, Roxie Goff, in starting a new chapter of her life. A life that involved matrimonial vows.

A life that seemed more distant and unreachable for Meredith as the years passed.

Meredith promptly quelled the feelings of jealousy not only of Roxie, but of all the other young brides who had come before Roxie, as well. These women were Meredith's friends. How could she even think of entertaining such covetous thoughts?

"Meredith, you have my dress!" Roxie, a younger version of her mother, rushed toward Meredith, her arms outstretched in anticipation. She offered to take the quilt-covered gown.

"I hope you like it."

"How could I not? You are only the best wedding dress seamstress west of the Mississippi."

Meredith laughed at her friend's proclamation. "I don't know if my legendary wedding dress skills are known from that great a distance."

"Of course, they are. I heard some women talking at the mercantile the other day about what exquisite dresses you sew. And I'm number nine, correct?"

Meredith took a deep breath. Nine dresses she had sewn for her friends and members of the Ellis Creek community. Nine dresses she had sewn for happy brides-to-be who had found the love of their dreams.

Would she herself ever know the joy of wearing such a dress?

With great care, Roxie removed the quilt from around the wedding dress. "It's breathtaking," she gasped.

"I'm thrilled you like it."

"Like it? I love it! May I try it?"

"Of course."

Meredith waited in the parlor while Roxie tried on her dress. Then, presenting herself for Mrs. Goff and Meredith, Roxie entered the parlor and twirled around as though a princess.

"Meredith, you really do fine work. Such a gift you have with the needle and thread," declared Mrs. Goff.

"Thank you, Mrs. Goff. It was my pleasure. After all, Roxie has been my best friend all these many years."

"And you have been such a dear friend to me as well." Roxie paused for a moment as if the realization Meredith had already contemplated finally settled in her heart, too. The thought that soon, after Roxie married Perry, things would change between them, and Roxie's time would be spent as that of a rancher's wife, and within a year, likely a mother.

Meredith pushed from her mind the speculation. She refused to let dismal thoughts ruin this special moment together with her best friend.

Roxie left the room and changed back into her everyday dress, all the while chatting about the wedding dress Meredith had sewn.

"Would you like some lemonade on the porch?" Roxie asked.

Meredith smiled. "That sounds delightful." How many times had she and Roxie shared lemonade on the Goff's porch? Too many to count.

Within moments, Roxie reappeared with two glasses of lemonade and took a seat beside Meredith. "Before you know it, you'll be stitching a wedding dress of your own, Meredith."

"That's decidedly unlikely." The words left her mouth before she could pay them any mind.

"God has someone planned for you, Meredith, I just know it."

"If you'll recall, I was the one everyone thought would marry first out of all of our friends, and by the age of eighteen, no less. Mind you, that definitely was not in God's plan."

"Who would guess that Idella would fall in love with Richard practically the day she met him during his visit to Ellis Creek?"

Meredith laughed. Idella and Richard had already been married nearly three years. They brought new proof to the old adage that love might just happen at first sight. "True. They do have a wonderful story to tell their daughter when she grows older."

"You do know that we will still be the best of friends, even after I marry Perry, right?"

"I know things will change, Roxie."

"They will change. Perry will be my main priority, after the Good Lord, of course. But we will still pay each other visits, chat about the goings-on of this town, and sit and drink lemonade on the porch. We haven't been friends for all these years to suddenly stop."

Meredith smiled at her dear friend. "You're right, Roxie. We shall remain grand friends, no matter what."

"True. And don't you let the fact that God hasn't sent the man He aims for you to marry bother you. His timing is different than our timing. Isn't that what the reverend always says?"

"Yes, and I know that the Lord knows and sees everything, but sometimes I wonder if He may have forgotten that in a few short months I'll be twenty-one years old. A spinster by any standard, especially in Ellis Creek."

"Fiddlesticks! The Montana Territory may be behind the times a bit. But in less than twenty years, we'll be entering a new century. Spinsterhood will be considered much later. Maybe even into a woman's mid-twenties."

"Well, whether or not that's true," said Meredith, taking a sip of her lemonade, "how can a girl find a man to marry when there are no options? And not just no options, but absolutely no options."

"Perhaps there are options we aren't seeing. Options right there before us."

"Please, Roxie, do give an example."

"Well, let's see. There's Mr. Griggs."

Meredith shivered at her friend's suggestion. "Mr. Griggs might be a worthwhile choice were it not for his lack of teeth and failure to bathe."

"I do suppose that Mr. Griggs is, shall we say, rather disheveled."

"Disheveled indeed."

"Mr. Norman from the post office would make a fine choice."

Meredith giggled at that suggestion. "If it wasn't that he is at least ninety years old."

"Marvin Pratt?"

Meredith held out her forefinger and thumb with only a small space between the two. "Only one inconsequential problem with Marvin Pratt: he will likely insist we live at his parents' home since he doesn't understand the verse in the Bible that states 'Therefore shall a man leave his father and his mother, and shall cleave unto his wife.'"

"Give poor Marvin time. He's only thirty."

"Any other suggestions, Roxie?"

"What about that new banker in town, Leopold Arkwright? He's quite sought after by some of the young women in Ellis Creek."

Meredith wrinkled her nose. The arrogant man had tried to court several of the young women in town, to no avail. "I dare say that Mr. Arkwright is quite one to put on airs. Also, wouldn't he be perturbed to know we weren't addressing him by his full name, Leopold Lawrence Arkwright, III?"

"He would indeed. But don't you find him the least bit dapper?" Roxie winked teasingly at her friend.

"Not in the least."

"He is one of the wealthiest men in Ellis Creek."

Meredith shrugged. "Riches are not all there is. Give me a poor man with a strong faith in the Lord and a kind and gracious nature over a wealthy one possessing Mr. Arkwright's personality any day."

"All right. I'll not press on about the notorious Leopold Lawrence Arkwright, III. Hmm." Roxie put her finger to her lips. "Gabe Kleeman?"

"Gabe Kleeman?"

"Yes, Lula's older brother?"

Meredith thought for a moment. Lula was the best friend of Meredith's younger sister, Tillie. Did Lula have a brother?

"Remember, Meredith, when we were in school? He was a head shorter than the rest of the boys—and the girls. A strong wind could blow him away, if I correctly recall."

"I think I remember him. Didn't he go to Minnesota to help his relatives?"

"Missouri, I believe."

"I recall he would retrieve Tillie from our home and from school on occasion. But it's been several years." Meredith pondered for a moment. "Oh, yes, I do vaguely recall him. Such a sickly fellow. It seemed he missed a lot of school."

"Yes, a nice boy, not like the others in school always pulling on our braids or teasing us." Roxie thoughtfully tapped her chin. "I do believe I heard from Mother, who heard from Mrs. Smith, who heard from Mrs. Plunkett, that Gabe has returned to Ellis Creek."

"I don't think there's anyone for me in Ellis Creek, Roxie. I may have to travel to the distant corners of the Montana Territory and beyond."

"Don't give up yet, Meredith. God has a plan."

Meredith offered a weak smile. She hoped God's plan didn't include spinsterhood.

## Chapter Two

GABE KLEEMAN STOOD IN the field and, turning, gazed in every direction. The Madison Range in the distance, the plentiful ranch land, and the numerous trees gave testimony to how blessed he was to have acquired such a fine piece of land. He couldn't have done it, of course, without Pa's help. Adjacent to his parents' property, the spread had come up for sale when the Potter family had moved to Iowa. Pa had suggested Gabe take out a loan on the property and start his own ranch.

From the beginning, that had been Gabe's dream—to own his own ranch.

Now, after three years, he was back in Ellis Creek. Not that he had minded traveling to Missouri to assist his aunt and uncle after his uncle's accident. The years spent there drew Gabe and his extended family closer, giving Gabe the opportunity to help ensure that his aunt and uncle didn't lose the farm they had worked so hard to keep.

God had answered the prayers of Gabe's entire family throughout the past couple of years. Gabe was stronger and healthier than he had ever been, and the days of his rough start in life as an ailing youngster would forever be in the past.

Gabe's return to Ellis Creek sealed the fact that he belonged here. Always had. His family, the land, the cattle, the beautiful summers, and the crisp winters would always beckon him to the place he had lived since a young lad. He had missed much since his time away and was glad to be back.

Three days later, Gabe sat in church awaiting the sermon. He hoped the reverend would preach another convicting sermon as he had done last week when he spoke of allowing God to take all your worries. The reverend had reiterated that the Lord cared for the smallest of sparrows. Gabe would need to remember that as he started this new chapter in his life operating his own ranch.

The Waller family sat in the fourth pew from the front. A fine location for the family in Gabe's humble estimate, as it afforded him ample time to take in the fine beauty of one Miss Meredith Waller. Not that Gabe wasn't listening to the goings-on at the church service and particularly the sermon, for indeed he was. But there was just something about the woman who had captured his attention all those years ago during their early school days. She hadn't known he existed then and she certainly didn't know now.

Meredith might never know if Gabe didn't figure out how to use the mouth God gave him to actually speak to her.

Old Mrs. Plunkett began playing a hymn on the piano and Gabe focused on his hymnal. When the song concluded, everyone took their seats to listen to the announcements. Out of the corner of his eye, Gabe had a perfect view of Meredith. Her long brown hair cascaded down her back in what Lula would call "ringlets." She had expressive pale blue eyes that he remembered from school when she appeared to be looking his way once. More like looking past him while in a daydream, but Gabe still recalled her sparkling eyes.

Meredith looked back over her shoulder, and Gabe redirected his attention to the front of the church. It wouldn't do to have Meredith discover he was staring at her. Did she even realize he had returned from Missouri? Had she even known he had left?

When Meredith faced forward again, Gabe's eyes wandered once again to gaze upon her beauty. What would she say if she ever knew he fancied her? Would she laugh? He had attempted once several years ago to speak to Meredith by asking her to a barn dance. When Gabe had finally forced the words from his mouth, he'd been horrified with embarrassment when he realized he had asked her to a *yarn bance.*

If only Gabe hadn't been born shy, maybe he would have a chance with the prettiest girl in Ellis Creek.

He could talk to just about everyone else in town, but when it came to Meredith, his tongue got tied into hopeless knots. Better not to say anything at all than embarrass himself again, as he had with the "yarn bance" incident.

A nudge to his ribcage drew his attention from Meredith to his younger sister sitting to his right. A sly look in her eyes told him he'd been caught. "What is it, Lula?" he whispered.

"I saw you."

"What?"

"I saw you staring at Meredith Waller. You are supposed to be listening to the announcements."

Gabe felt the warmth travel up his neck. He shook his head. Why was it that his parents decided to have another child when Gabe was ten? Couldn't he have remained an only child? Not that he didn't love Lula with all his being, but a pesky sort she was, especially at times like these.

"I could listen if you weren't talking."

Lula narrowed her eyes at him. "I know you fancy Meredith Waller."

"She seems nice enough."

"Maybe I should tell Tillie."

"You wouldn't dare."

Lula merely shrugged, her long brown braids bobbing as she did. She stuck her chin out and focused her attention on the reverend, acting as though she had been listening intently to the announcements all along.

In all his shyness, and there was plenty of it, Gabe would die an early death if Lula ever breathed a word of her suspicions. He would have to purchase more of those jawbreakers she had grown so fond of and bribe her with one each week to keep her conjectures to herself.

## Chapter Three

TILLIE WALLER COULDN'T WAIT until recess to speak with her best friend, Lula Kleeman. If lunch recess didn't arrive soon, she might be forced to sneak over to Lula's desk during arithmetic and let her know all about the grand plan she had concocted in her head while doing her chores last night.

But that would never do. Miss Apgar would tan her hide for sure if Tillie dared speak out of turn in class.

So instead, Tillie sat, attempting to do her best at listening to reasons why she had to learn double-digit multiplication, although Miss Apgar's reasons clearly lacked merit. Tillie prided herself on being more of a word-girl than a number-girl.

She removed her spectacles and rubbed her tired eyes. Arithmetic had a way of boring her. If she lasted the next hour without drifting into a deep sleep, it would be nothing short of miraculous. Tillie quietly drummed her fingers on the desk and every so often glanced Lula's way, hoping to catch her eye.

Finally, after what seemed like a multitude of hours, Miss Apgar announced that lunch recess had arrived. "Now pupils, as always, please eat your lunch first, then play."

Tillie and the rest of the students chorused, "Yes, ma'am." For as smart as Miss Apgar was, she certainly never provided a variety of words to her standard "eat first then play" speech.

All of the students clamored for their tin pails on the shelf in the back of the classroom with youngest going first and elders toward the back. Tillie tapped her toe on the floor, attempting her best to be patient. Finally, her turn came, and she grabbed her tin pail and bolted out the door.

"Lula!"

"Tillie!"

The two embraced as if they hadn't seen each other just yesterday. Such was the case with best friends, Tillie supposed.

"I have the grandest plan in all the West."

Lula stared at Tillie with wide eyes. "Really?"

"Yes, I must tell you or I fear I shall be unable to endure the rest of the day."

"Let's go sit under the tree and you can tell me all about it."

Tillie followed Lula to the large tree at the edge of the schoolyard. "What is it?" Lula inquired.

"You know how you and I were discussing that your brother is so lonely since returning from Missouri and that my sister is so distraught over everyone else having a beau?"

Lula removed a sandwich from her tin pail. "Yes?"

"Well, while I was doing chores last night, I had the most splendid plan."

"Do tell!"

"Why don't we arrange for your brother and my sister to fall in love?" Finally, Tillie had set free the words of her heart. Surely Lula would see the importance of the plan, just as Tillie had when the idea had popped into her head.

"Do people arrange for people to fall in love?" Lula asked.

"Well, sure."

"All right. So what is your plan?"

Tillie placed her apple back in her tin pail. Who could eat at a time like this? "I'm glad you asked, Lula. You see, we could write love letters."

"Love letters? Wherever did you ever get that idea?"

"I overheard Mama telling Papa that during the War, Grandmother and Grandfather wrote letters back and forth to stay in touch. Mama said that Grandmother was a fright, wondering if Grandfather would return from fighting for the North unscathed."

"You and your big words, Tillie."

"That's why I do well in writing, but not in arithmetic. Anyhow, we write love letters and soon Meredith and Gabe fall in love, get married, and we'll be sisters forever."

Lula absentmindedly placed a finger to her lips, seemingly pondering the thought. Tillie had known her best friend since they were little. She just knew Lula would see the importance of such an endeavor.

"We're only eleven. How could we possibly help two people fall in love?" Lula asked.

"It's been done before. Besides, we'll both be twelve soon."

"How do we deliver the letters to them?"

Tillie scrunched her nose. "I hadn't thought of that yet. I only thought about composing the letters." She refused to allow this complication to hinder her plans. "There has to be a way. Say, what about mailing the letters?"

"That would get mighty pricey. Have you seen the price of a stamp lately?"

"True. Perhaps we could ask someone to deliver the letters for us."

"And risk that person telling either Gabe or Meredith that we are behind this scheme?"

"Lula, you are always so pragmatic." Couldn't Lula be a dreamer like herself, just once?

"Not pragmatic, just realistic. We mustn't allow anyone to find out it is us writing the letters. Our plan would never work then."

"There has to be a way." Tillie decided just this once to eat her dessert before her sandwich. Taking a bite of her cookie, she closed her eyes in quick prayer. Surely, the Lord saw the importance of the situation, didn't He?

"Are you sure Gabe and Meredith want to fall in love?"

"They do. They just don't know it yet." Tillie spoke with her mouth full of cookie, glad that Mama wasn't around to witness her appalling breach of manners.

"I've never heard Gabe say he wants to fall in love."

"Do boys even talk about such things?"

Lula shook her head. "Not that I know of. You have a brother. Does he ever swoon over any girls in town?"

"Charles is a scatterbrain. All he thinks about is hunting and catching fish. His days are boring to say the least. But he's only 15. In time, he'll realize the importance of falling in love. Meredith is different." Tillie leaned in toward Lula and reduced her voice to a whisper. "Don't tell anyone, but I heard her sniffling a bit when she was finishing Roxie's wedding dress."

"Perhaps there was dust in the air. Maybe she wasn't sad at all."

"Oh, she was distraught all right. She kept pulling the dress toward herself, and I could see the wistful gaze in her eyes."

Lula shot a suspicious glance Tillie's way. All right, so maybe there was dust in the air and maybe Meredith's wistful gaze was because she would not be spending as much time with Roxie as they had in the past once Roxie married Perry. Tillie had overheard Mama and Meredith speaking about how things change once a woman marries and her husband takes top priority in her life. But Tillie wouldn't admit all of that to Lula.

"Gabe is content running his new ranch. I don't think he cares about—wait a minute. I did happen to see him staring at Meredith at church Sunday."

"Really?"

"Are you thinking what I'm thinking, Tillie?"

"And are you thinking what I'm thinking, Lula?"

Both girls nodded. "We must arrange for them to fall in love," Tillie proclaimed.

"A most excellent plan indeed! When do we start?"

"Tomorrow. Tonight, we will each come up with a plan on how to deliver the letters and how best to keep this a secret."

"And," added Lula, "what to write in those letters."

Tillie pointed her thumb at herself. "You leave that to me."

The following day at lunch recess, the plans were in place to arrange a falling-in-love between Meredith Waller and Gabe Kleeman.

"We mail the first letter to Meredith," Lula announced.

"Do we have two cents for the stamp?"

"I have a penny saved. If we can come up with another penny, this plan could very well work."

"I have a penny."

Lula grinned. "Perfect. But I haven't an idea about the rest of the letters. We need to write several back and forth."

They had come this far. They couldn't let this minor obstacle block their path. "I know!" Tillie announced. "We can hide the letters in that sliver of a space behind the big knot on that huge oak tree at the edge of town, just past the Jones' place. It would be a perfect hiding place. We can tell Meredith in her first letter that each letter thereafter will be at the tree. She can place her return letters to Gabe there as well. It's an excellent hiding place if no squirrels haul off the letter, and no one in town will know since the tree is off of the main road."

"Yes, but you forgot something."

"What's that?" Tillie panicked. What of her well-planned idea?

"You forgot that Gabe is a boy. Do boys even like writing letters?"

"Some must. Our McGuffey Readers were written by William Holmes McGuffey, who was a man. Or look at Noah Webster. His dictionary is one of my favorite books of all time."

"True. But...Gabe is neither Mr. McGuffey nor Mr. Webster, and I'm not sure Gabe will be all right with the idea. He might be embarrassed. He's a reticent fellow, after all."

"That is true." Tillie bit her lip and pondered their latest hindrance. "I have a splendid idea! Why don't we write the letters for Gabe? At least until he warms to the idea, then he can begin writing his own."

"When do we tell him?"

"After ten letters at least."

"When do we start?"

"We'll write our first letter right now. It won't do for me to pen it, as Meredith will recognize my penmanship, so you'll have to accomplish that task. This will meet with imminent success. I can feel it in my bones, as Grandmama Waller would say." The contents of the letter began to crowd her mind.

"This is quite thrilling. Can you imagine if our plan works? I declare the way Gabe stared at Meredith in church could put us one step closer to being sisters forever."

This truly was more exciting than just about anything Tillie had experienced as of late. She removed a piece of writing paper that she had pilfered from Meredith's stationery pile, and together, she and Lula wrote the first of several letters.

After all, if they couldn't discover a new world like Christopher Columbus or sew the American flag like Betsy Ross, they could certainly make a difference for all humanity in their own small way.

## Chapter Four

NOT SINCE MEREDITH HAD corresponded with Grandmama had she received any mail. When Mr. Norman waved her down on the boardwalk, she thought he must be mistaken. "Miss Waller, I have a letter for you!"

Perhaps the letter was for Mama. Meredith turned and started toward the elderly postmaster.

"This here came for you just today." Mr. Norman held the envelope in his wrinkled hand.

Arching an eyebrow, Meredith took the letter. "Thank you, Mr. Norman. It isn't often that I receive mail."

"I always feel like I'm giving folks a Christmas present. Unless, of course, the letter is bad news." Mr. Norman grinned, his aged face showing his years. "Am I to assume you have received good news, Miss Waller?"

Meredith turned the letter over in her hands. She didn't recognize the penmanship. "I do hope it is good news, Mr. Norman. I'm not expecting anything to the contrary."

"Well, I'll leave you be then to open your letter. Tell your folks I said 'hello.'"

"I will, Mr. Norman. Thank you."

Mr. Norman waved and ambled back to the post office.

Meredith claimed a bench outside of the mercantile to open her letter. The stationery looked rather familiar, like her own cream-colored writing paper. The two-cent stamp had been placed rather haphazardly and crooked in the corner.

Who could be sending her a letter?

She carefully opened the seal and unfolded the ivory sheet of paper. Her eyes traveled across the words, not once, not twice, but three times:

*Dear Miss Waller,*
*It has taken me considerable courage to write to you. I believe you are not only lovely, but also kind and charitable.*

*Yours Truly,*
*Your Secret Admirer*

*P.S. If you would like to write back and forth, please check the sliver of a space behind the big knot on that huge oak tree at the edge of town, just past the Jones's place. I will place another letter there for you in the coming week.*

Meredith shook her head. Was the letter written in jest? She looked around at all the people walking up and down the street, down the boardwalk, and into the stores. Who in Ellis Creek would send her such a letter? And did she want to write back and forth? How could she if she didn't even know who had sent the letter?

On the other hand, she allowed herself, just for a moment, to believe that someone really did find her lovely, kind, and charitable. A handsome prince of sorts, only in the modern times of 1884. As quickly as the thought entered her mind, she dismissed it. For who in Ellis Creek was a handsome prince? And who in Ellis Creek would call her lovely, kind, and charitable, and wish to write to her? Perhaps the writer of the letter hailed from another town in the Montana Territory or beyond. If so, how had he known to write to her? How did he even know her?

Questions filled her mind in rapid order, as she folded the letter and returned it to its envelope. One thing was for certain: she aimed to discover the author.

Meredith removed the pan of biscuits from the oven. Mama had invited the Kleeman family over for supper, thinking it a good idea and adding that it was the perfect way for them to welcome Gabe Kleeman back to Ellis Creek after his time in Missouri. Meredith hadn't seen Gabe in at least three years, possibly longer. In her mind, he was the very same boy Roxie spoke of in their conversation a few days ago. Puny in stature, sickly, and shy. The poor man. Had he improved in health? Meredith recalled someone, Mama maybe, mentioning that Gabe Kleeman hadn't been healthy as a child due to a long illness.

Mama, Meredith, and Tillie set the table while Papa and Charles finished the outside chores. Before long, the Kleemans arrived at the front door. Mama and Mrs. Kleeman eagerly greeted each other as if they hadn't just seen each other in church a few days ago. Tillie and Lula squealed in exuberance and immediately began whispering and giggling. Mr. Kleeman shook Papa's hand and talk of the prices of cattle began.

Meredith was about to shut the door when a large foot blocked the door, causing her to jump back in surprise. "I'm so sorry! I didn't see you there." Her face was just inches from that of a young man in the doorway. One of those salesman touting fake remedies that had been rumored to be arriving in Ellis Creek, perhaps?

"May I help you?" Meredith asked.

The man fiddled with the button on his shirt cuff. "Uh, I'm Gabe Kleeman."

"Gabe Kleeman?"

"My family... was... invited over for supper."

A flush found its way up Meredith's neck. *How embarrassing! Could I just disappear now and avoid this whole humiliating course of circumstances?* "I'm so sorry, Mr. Kleeman. Do come in."

While opening the door, Meredith stumbled back, nearly losing her footing. Gabe Kleeman stepped through the door as she eyed him with suspicion. Where was the puny, sickly, small-statured boy she recalled from school?

Mama rushed toward the young Mr. Kleeman. "It's so nice to have you back in Ellis Creek, Gabe. We can't wait to hear about your time in Missouri."

"Thank you, Mrs. Waller, for the supper invitation." Gabe Kleeman took a seat at the table next to Charles.

"I heard you've been back about a week." Pa said.

"Yes, sir."

Meredith assisted Mama with the remaining food, then took her seat next to Tillie and across from Gabe Kleeman. The humiliation of nearly shutting the man's foot in the door still flooded her mind. What must he think of her? Thankfully, no one else in either family seemed to have noticed.

Pa said the blessing, thanking the Lord for the meal. Commotion then ensued as food was passed and plates heaped. "How was Missouri, Gabe?" Mama asked.

"I was thankful for the opportunity to be able to help my aunt and uncle." Gabe moved some green beans on his plate with his fork, maintaining eye contact with Mama. "Reckon I am glad to be back, though."

"We are so glad to have him back," said Mrs. Kleeman. "Gabe has purchased some land just west of ours and is going to have his own ranch."

"That's wonderful." Mama buttered a piece of biscuit. "We are so proud of you, Gabe."

Meredith watched Gabe nod, seemingly nervous, at Mama's outburst of excitement. But then, Mama was nearly always excited about something. Pa said that was one of the things he loved about her the most—her cheerful fuss over everything from big things to seemingly mundane things. Gabe shifted in his seat and pushed more green beans to the side of his plate. The poor guy radiated nervousness under all the scrutiny.

"I see Tillie often, but, Meredith, how are you doing, dear?" Mrs. Kleeman asked.

"I am well, thank you."

Mama beamed, her smile lighting up her entire face. "Meredith sewed another wedding dress, this time for Roxie Goff. She is getting quite well-known for her elegant creations."

"That is just delightful, dear. Perhaps someday you will sew one for yourself," Mrs. Kleeman said.

While there was no unkindness in her words, Meredith wanted to shrink beneath the table all the same. Why did everyone make such a fuss about her spinsterhood? "Yes, maybe so," she squeaked. Or maybe not.

The letter she'd received in the mail entered her mind, and she brushed the thought aside. That one lonely letter could hardly be considered an auspicious foretelling of her marital future.

The conversation turned to Tillie and Lula and their schooling. Meredith took a deep breath and sent a prayer of thanks to the good Lord for His provision in allowing the supper-table discussion to turn from her. Meredith needn't be reminded of the imminent arrival of spinsterhood and the immense distress it caused her.

She took a bite of meatloaf and caught Gabe Kleeman's gaze as it connected with hers. An unexpected shiver traveled through her. Mr. Kleeman hurriedly looked away, his nicely-shaped ears turning red.

Nicely-shaped ears? Where had that silly notion come from? Sure, the young Mr. Kleeman did have nice ears, a nice face too, but why was she noticing? And how had a man changed so much in the past three years? Puny did not enter the description of this now over six-foot-tall man with strong arms.

Meredith had never been considered shy. Quite the opposite, actually. She was a lot like Mama in her outgoing nature, although more realistic. Sitting here at the table with the changed Gabe Kleeman, however, did something to her insides she couldn't quite explain.

Gabe found sleep difficult that night. He tossed and turned, thinking of Meredith Waller and her pretty face across from him at the dinner table. He beheld in his mind the way a few strands of loose hair, the color of freshly upturned topsoil, hung around her shoulders. Her blue eyes had glinted every time she spoke and Gabe had tried not to stare.

She had almost shut his foot in the door, not that Gabe minded. For a chance to court her, he would allow Meredith to shut his foot—both of his feet—in the door once a day if she desired. If only there was some way to make his intentions known. If only there was some way to know if she'd ever feel the same for him as he felt for her.

He deemed admiring Meredith Waller from a distance much safer.

Sure, Gabe was shy toward a few people, but he did quite well articulating his thoughts to those he had known for a good portion of his life. With Meredith, however, the words barely rose past his throat. She likely thought him a bumbling fool. Ma would remind him that muttering wasn't gentlemanly, and Gabe would chastise himself once again for his apprehensive disposition.

God had richly blessed Gabe with a loving family, a good-sized spread of a ranch, and, after so many years, the healing of his body. Gabe would never take good health for granted, not after having lived as an unhealthy boy without the ability to walk far without tiring, only to become a robust man with energy to spare.

*Lord, I reckon this is a bit out of the ordinary, but could You please help me find words to speak to Meredith? And if it's Your will, Lord, might I ask that she be favorable toward me?*

## Chapter Five

THE SECOND LETTER ARRIVED a week later. Meredith had checked the hole in the tree every day, not that she'd admit to anyone her curious obsession with an old tree on the way to town. Or why she made numerous trips to town when she had more important matters to tend to.

She scrutinized the obscure writing that she recognized from the prior letter. Her heart thumped loudly as she unfolded the letter:

*Dear Miss Waller,*
*The rose is red, the violet's blue,*

*The honey's sweet, and so are you.*
*Yours Truly,*
*Your Secret Admirer*

Meredith blushed at the words. Yes, she knew they weren't original, but to have been copied by this mysterious secret admirer's hand and placed in the tree thrilled her.

Reaching into her reticule, Meredith retrieved her own envelope. Opening the flap, she read it one last time before depositing it in the secret place in the tree:

*Dear Secret Admirer,*
*Thank you for your kind letters. Can you give me a hint as to your identity? Are you from Ellis Creek? Elsewhere in the Montana Territory? Do I know you? How do you know me?*
*Yours Truly,*
*Meredith Waller*

Perhaps she had asked too many questions. What would etiquette books say of her superfluous curiosity?

At the notion of the etiquette books addressing the topic of conversing by letter with a secret admirer, Meredith laughed. Perhaps she should pen her own etiquette book and discuss such an unorthodox topic.

Weighing her options, Meredith finally persuaded herself to place the letter in the tree. If the questions in her letter were answered, the list of names Meredith had compiled for possibilities could be considerably narrowed.

Not that her mental list proved lengthy. No, it contained just four possibilities: Leopold Arkwright, Mr. Griggs, Marvin Pratt, and an unnamed, unknown man from outside Ellis Creek. Not good choices. Well, except for the man from outside of Ellis Creek; he could have potential.

Meredith sighed. Maybe she didn't want to know the identity of her mysterious suitor, after all.

Meredith slowed the wagon in front of the home of Widow Jones. A humble home, the one-story whitewashed house provided just enough room for the widow and her two young grandchildren.

Clutching her basket of sewing in one hand and two loaves of bread in the other, Meredith prayed she would bless the widow who had lost her beloved husband of 50 years and her son and daughter-in-law all in a year's time.

"Widow Jones?" Meredith called while tapping on the door.

"Meredith, what a delight to see you." With fingers gnarled from painful arthritis, Widow Jones opened the door and beckoned Meredith to enter.

"I brought your mending and two loaves of Mama's bread, fresh out of the oven."

Widow Jones smiled, bringing more prominence to the fine wrinkles that lined her soft face. "You are a dear, Meredith. Do come in."

Meredith followed Widow Jones into the home, placing the loaves of bread on the table. She reached a hand toward the widow's shawl-covered arm. "How are you doing today?"

"I am blessed. I don't know what I'd do without the Body of Christ," Widow Jones continued. "You have all been so gracious to me in my time of need. How do people go through rough times without Jesus and the ones He calls to help us?"

Meredith and the widow chatted for some time until a knock at the door interrupted their conversation. "I wonder who could be paying me a visit. Would you mind seeing for me, Meredith? Getting out of this chair is a mite difficult anymore."

Meredith opened the front door to see none other than Gabe Kleeman. For a moment, her heart left her at the sight of the man before her. "Mr. Kleeman, what brings you here on this fine day? Do come in."

Gabe Kleeman had a nervous way about him and avoided her gaze. He appeared as though he wanted to say something, but couldn't quite find the words. Instead, he nodded at Meredith and followed her into the widow's home.

"Gabe, is that you?" Widow Jones called.

"Yes, Widow Jones, it is."

Meredith observed that the handsome man had found his voice. He walked toward the widow, a crate in his arms. Arms with sleeves rolled up to his elbows and showing fibrous, sinewy muscles in his forearms.

Not that Meredith noticed.

Because Gabe Kleeman certainly didn't notice her at all. Not one bit.

"Ma wanted me to deliver a jar of jam and some spuds. I thought I'd also mend that fence while I'm here."

"You are such a dear, Gabe. That would be delightful. Before you mend the fence, why don't you join Meredith and me for some of your ma's jam on her mama's delicious bread?"

"Reckon that sounds fine, Widow Jones." Gabe sauntered toward the table where he set the crate. "Nice day outside. Perhaps I could assist you outside on the porch for some sunshine."

Feeling a bit left out of the conversation, Meredith set about slicing three pieces of bread. Then, standing near Mr. Kleeman, she waited for the right moment to inquire if she might unload the jar of jam from the crate he still hovered over.

"That would be resplendent, Gabe. Perhaps we could carry this chair to the porch." Widow Jones patted the arms of the rocking chair.

"No need for that, ma'am. I brought a chair for you in the back of my wagon."

Widow Jones's eyes grew wide. "You brought a chair for me to borrow? An outside chair?"

"Better than that. I made you a chair you can keep. That way, you can keep watch over your grandsons while they do their chores or play outside."

"My, but isn't he a fine young man, Meredith?" Widow Jones beamed. "A handsome one at that."

Meredith didn't have to have Mama's handheld mirror to know her face was covered with a bright red blush.

The tips of Gabe Kleeman's ears grew red and he glanced at her out of the corner of his eye. The poor man must be just as embarrassed.

Meredith cleared her throat in the most ladylike way possible. "Mr. Kleeman, might I have the jar of jam? I'll prepare each of us a slice of bread." There. She had changed the subject. Now she would will her face, likely the color of the strawberry preserves in Gabe Kleeman's crate, to return to a normal pallor.

Mr. Kleeman nodded and reached into the crate for a jar of jam. He turned, and without meeting her eye, handed it to her.

Only something happened and the jar didn't make its graceful transition from Mr. Kleeman's hand to Meredith's. Instead, it began a quick descent to the floor.

With agile and nimble fingers, Gabe Kleeman caught and rescued the jam before it splattered all over Widow Jones's floor.

Meredith released the breath she was holding as Mr. Kleeman returned to his normal height. "Here, uh, Miss Waller," he muttered, handing her the jar.

When his fingers lightly brushed hers, Meredith almost dropped the jar of preserves all over again. "Thank you."

Gabe Kleeman's eyes darted from Meredith's face to some unknown spot on the wall behind her. Did he blame her for the awkward transition of the jam jar? Meredith hastily found an empty space on the table and continued her preparations. She inhaled the delectable scent of the strawberry preserves and attempted her best to forget that Mr. Kleeman stood nearby.

"Meredith, don't you and Gabe know each other from your school days?" Widow Jones asked.

Meredith almost jumped plumb out of her skin at the widow's voice. "Begging your pardon, Widow Jones?"

"Are not you and Gabe acquaintances from school?"

Meredith attempted to reconcile the puny and feeble boy she remembered from school with the strong and healthy man not far from her side. "Yes, ma'am, we are."

"And don't you two know each other from church, Gabe?" Widow Jones questioned.

"Yes, Widow, we do."

"Then why is it that you are both so formal? Mr. Kleeman this, Miss Waller that. Ellis Creek is a small town. Now, I understand calling older folks by their surnames and with all the politeness your mamas taught you, but you two are young folks and have known each other nearly all of your lives. Why not just forego the Waller and Kleeman notions and make good use of your given names?"

"Yes, ma'am," Meredith and Gabe chorused.

Meredith mused that calling Mr. Kleeman "Gabe" would be so much easier if he knew she existed. Liking him from afar was a challenge.

Would he ever notice her?

She might just have to give up on that quest if shutting his foot in the door and clumsily dropping jam hadn't worked.

Gabe started his work on the fence, all the while knowing that the beautiful woman of his affections stood nearby on the porch as Widow Jones sat in her new chair. If only he had made a good impression on her. Instead, his fumble fingers had almost dropped the jar of preserves. What must Meredith think of him?

He could hear her sunny laughter as Meredith and the widow conversed. With a squint of his eyes from the sun, Gabe caught a glimpse of her slender form. Meredith was taller than most women, but he wagered—no he knew—that the top of Meredith's head reached his chin. If she tilted her pretty little head back just right, he could plant a kiss atop those lips without even having to bend much.

*Whoa, Gabe Kleeman. Back up the horse.* What kind of thoughts were those? That he could kiss her without even bending much? Gabe shook his head. He had no business thinking such thoughts, especially about a woman who didn't and wouldn't likely ever know of his affections.

But then, he couldn't just tell her of his fondness for her. Not when his tongue either didn't work or was tied up in knots at the very sight of her. It happened each time Gabe was in her presence. His knees shook beneath his trousers, he had a strong desire to run in the opposite direction, and words that formed in his throat never made it to his mouth.

He wished beyond wishes the Good Lord hadn't made him so shy. Gabe could have done with just a minute bit of the boldness God gave other men.

Standing so close to her in the widow's house had almost been his undoing. When the jar of jam nearly fell and then his fingers brushed hers—was this what it felt like to be in love?

*Fiddlesticks!* What was a man doing thinking of such things anyway? He would be laughed all the way to a water-filled trough where he'd be dunked for sure in a quest to empty his head of such foolish notions.

Gabe glimpsed a moment into his far-off future. He would be 90 years old and still eyeing Meredith from a distance. His voice would crackle with age—not that many words would leave his lips when in Meredith's presence. Meredith would have white hair like Widow

Jones and wrinkles aplenty, yet he'd still find her easy on the eyes. And while Gabe would have likely lost all his teeth and his eyesight would be starting to deteriorate, things would still be the same in one way: his admiration for Meredith would remain.

In the middle of mending the fence, a thought occurred to Gabe. Should he retrieve a chair for Meredith from the house? Surely, she would enjoy sitting with Widow Jones on the porch. And if Meredith continued to stay on the porch in a comfortable chair, Gabe could admire her all the more. From a safe distance, of course.

Gabe rolled his eyes. When had he become a lovelorn fool? He had never been able to speak to Meredith at school on the rare days when he'd attended. He'd missed so many days from illness, having to partake in studies in his bed or, when feeling better, at the kitchen table. When he attended school, Gabe took to staring at Meredith when she was facing the opposite direction. She never knew, not once, that he had admired her from the back of the schoolroom. She also never knew that he was the one who'd brought her a fresh apple from the neighbor's apple tree and placed it at her desk at school. She'd thought for sure it was that obnoxious Dean Floshour.

Years later, Gabe's feelings for Meredith endured. He sighed and sauntered toward the house. Even if he couldn't find the words to speak to her, he could be a gentleman. His ma had raised him right.

"Gabe, dear. This chair is right comfortable. Thank you for making it for me. Isn't Gabe a fine carpenter, Meredith?"

"Indeed, he is, Widow Jones." Of course, Meredith would be polite and agree with the widow, even if Gabe had built a shabby and ill-constructed chair.

"I was wondering if—" Gabe took a deep breath, and instead of addressing his question to Meredith, he took the safer route and addressed Widow Jones. "I was wondering, Widow, if I might retrieve a chair for Miss Wal—Meredith from the house so she might sit with you, rather than stand."

"Sounds right fine, Gabe. Although I must insist you ask her if she would desire a chair."

Gabe was afraid of that. Perhaps he should retreat back to the field. The fence wouldn't mend itself. He glanced back at the field. It wasn't that far and since Meredith likely thought him a fool, it would hardly strike her as odd if he retreated without directly asking her.

"Go ahead, Gabe. Ask her," Widow Jones prodded. The kindly old woman sure didn't help matters much.

"Uh, Meredith?"

"Yes?"

If only he could have continued without her gazing up at him with those sparkly blue eyes. Suddenly, he lost all nerve.

If he'd ever had any to begin with.

Silence filled the air. Gabe looked away. He focused his attention on the mountains, the ground, the corral, and then the barn. Finally, he had a solution to his dilemma. Sauntering past Meredith and Widow Jones, he entered the home, retrieved the chair, and set it next to the widow's chair.

Meredith threw him an odd glance. "Thank you, Gabe," she said, taking a seat on the house chair.

Gabe touched the brim of his hat, hurrying back to mending the fence. He shook his head. Whatever would Meredith think of him now?

Meredith took a seat on the house chair and watched as Gabe returned to the field. Had she done something to offend him? He certainly seemed peculiar and hesitant around her. He rarely looked her in the eye and he spoke less often than that. Maybe his illness had rendered him unable to speak many words.

Then why did he have no problem speaking to others? Meredith shrugged. The man perplexed her.

"That Gabe must not be feeling well. He is usually chattier than that," Widow Jones said, interrupting Meredith's thoughts. "It's so nice having him back in Ellis Creek. What with him helping his aunt and uncle in Missouri for those years, I know his family here missed him something awful. Can you believe how much healthier he looks?"

Meredith turned her face to avoid allowing Widow Jones a chance to see her flushed expression. Gabe looked healthy, alright. Downright handsome with those brawny shoulders.

Widow Jones continued. "I recall how burdensome it was for him always feeling poorly as a young'un. Here about four or five years ago, he started to feel much better. Do you remember that?"

"I'm sorry, I don't, Widow Jones." Where had she been, for goodness' sake, that she could not remember even seeing much of Gabe? Meredith recalled him in school, but then as they got older, she hadn't seen as much of him, even though their parents and their sisters were friends.

"Then he goes to Missouri and breathes in that fresh Midwestern air and the Lord heals him, what appears to be completely. Can't anyone say the Lord doesn't perform miracles anymore. Look what our gracious Father did for Gabe." Widow Jones held out her gnarled fingers. "I'm praying for a miracle with this arthritis."

*The topic of conversation needs to be changed from the discussion of Gabe.* "Widow Jones, you know I aim to be of assistance to you with the sewing or baking or whatever else you need, as is my mama."

"Yes, and I thank you kindly for that. Now back to Gabe."

*So much for changing the subject*, thought Meredith. "Such a fine man. Do you know if he's entered into a courtship with anyone in Ellis Creek?" Widow Jones scrutinized Meredith, seemingly prying for details.

Meredith swallowed hard and prayed that Widow Jones missed the rosy tint that dotted her face. "I can't say as I know for sure, ma'am." "Perhaps you ought to ponder such a thought yourself. You'd make a right fine couple. And what's there not to like about that young man out there mending my fence? A godly, kind soul if there ever was one."

"That he is, Widow Jones."

Meredith chastised herself for hoping that the eyesight of Widow Jones wasn't what it had once been. Otherwise, the elderly woman would see the embarrassment Meredith found impossible to disguise.

# Chapter Six

MEREDITH HADN'T RECEIVED A letter from her secret admirer in over three days. Disappointed, she decided to walk to church ahead of the rest of her family to check the tree for a letter and, of course, get some fresh air. Thankfully, Tillie hadn't suggested Meredith needed a little sister to join her on that walk.

When Meredith reached the tree, she eyed the surrounding area, reassuring herself there were no onlookers. For what would one think about Meredith Waller reaching into an old tree to claim personal letters? That latest piece of gossip would ripple through Ellis Creek in less than five minutes.

Sure enough, an envelope with the same writing had been placed in the tree. Taking several steps away from the tree, Meredith promptly opened it:

*Dear Miss Waller,*
*Thank you for writing me and for your questions. I am somewhat from Ellis Creek. Yes, you know me. Yes, I know you. I hope you are having a splendid week. Are you going to the church potluck?*
*Yours Truly,*
*Your Secret Admirer*

When had the author delivered this most recent letter? Would he be attending the potluck today after church? For that matter, did he attend church?

He mentioned that they knew each other. Meredith's brow furrowed. He had answered all of her questions, although the answer about his residence bordered on obscurity. *Somewhat from Ellis Creek?*

Such revelations could only mean one of two things. Either her secret admirer was indeed Mr. Griggs, Leopold Arkwright, or Marvin Pratt, although none of these choices held even the least bit of appeal. Or Meredith's admirer could be someone she hadn't yet considered.

Meredith chose the latter scenario.

Reaching into her reticule, she placed another letter in the tree. She had to have hope. Otherwise, this constant writing back and forth was futile.

The church potluck followed the service and Meredith watched as her parents joined with friends. Tillie, Lula, and Charles bounded toward their classmates, and the group Mama had termed "the young folks" met on the east side of the church. Meredith headed toward the group, many of whom she had known since childhood.

Soon-to-be-married Roxie and Perry joined other young couples, including Idella and Richard and Enid and Hugh. Meredith felt a bit out of place with all the other couples either already married or courting, but took comfort when she saw Gabe. *Thank you, Lord, that I am not the only one without someone.* Her eyes connected with Gabe's for a brief moment before he looked away. Could that have been a slight twinge of a smile on his lips?

Greetings took place around the circle of friends and conversation began. *Perhaps this won't be so bad after all*, Meredith thought, engaging herself in talk with her female friends about the newest fabric patterns at the mercantile.

They stood in line for their food, then regrouped, sitting on the grass. Meredith thought perhaps her heart might thump right out of her chest when Gabe took a seat next to her on her left.

What if she dribbled lemonade down her chin or plopped a piece of pie right in her lap with the object of her affection sitting so close? A surreptitious glimpse at Gabe's strong profile told her he might be just as nervous as she.

Roxie sat to her immediate right. "What a perfect day for a potluck," her best friend exclaimed in between bites of her sandwich. "Oh, look. There's Widow Jones."

The group waved at the widow and her young grandsons, as they headed toward friends. "Were you able to convince Widow Jones to allow you to assist her with her mending, Meredith?" Enid asked. "Ma says the widow can be a bit stubborn at times."

"I was. Her arthritis is so painful sometimes. I told her I was happy to retrieve her mending once a week, or more often if need be." Meredith saw Hugh shoot a mischievous glance toward Gabe.

"I hear that you and Meredith were out helping the Widow on the same day last week," Hugh said, a smirk lining his dark features. Hugh had always had a wit about him. Meredith just wished this time it hadn't been directed toward her and Gabe and the irony of their visit to Widow Jones on the same day. Thank goodness Hugh hadn't been there to observe the falling jam jar episode.

"Yes. I mended a fence for her," said Gabe.

"So you and Meredith were able to assist the Widow on the same day. That's good." Hugh nudged Enid and they gave each other a knowing glance.

Meredith knew her cheeks had to be the color of the red flowers on her calico skirt and from her peripheral view, she saw Gabe shift to a different sitting position.

The conversation soon changed to another topic and Meredith attempted to relax. Suddenly, a strong gust of wind blew, causing Meredith's handkerchief to float from her lap.

She leaned forward to retrieve it.

Gabe did the same.

Their heads connected with a clunk and Meredith winced.

"I'm…sorry, Meredith," Gabe whispered.

When Meredith opened her eyes, Gabe's face was directly in front of hers. Their eyes connected. His, so handsomely hazel. And then with that lock of brown hair falling over his forehead…Meredith knew her heart stopped for certain. The awkwardness of the situation hampered her breathing, and she stared into his eyes, and he into hers. For a moment, she forgot all about the threatening headache from the collision with Gabe's noggin.

Several chuckles and giggles interrupted Meredith's whimsical thoughts and she and Gabe hastily pulled away from each other. Meredith placed a hand on the sore spot of her head.

Silence ensued. All of their friends waiting to see what happened next in this awkward, yet romantic situation, perhaps? Meredith inwardly cringed. She'd never hear the end of it from Roxie, Enid, and Idella.

"Sorry," Gabe said.

"Begging your pardon," squeaked Meredith, their words colliding in chorus.

"Here." He handed her the handkerchief that had caused all the troubles in the first place. She attempted to reclaim the handkerchief, only to miss it and have it drift to the ground in front of her. Careful not to have a repeat of their heads colliding, Gabe cautiously picked up the handkerchief and again handed it to her.

"Goodness, but I fear I have butterfingers today." Meredith found it odd that her voice sounded like someone else's entirely in her ears, all high-pitched and shrill. Since when was she so antsy?

When the dapper Gabe Kleeman was sitting within a foot of her, that's when.

Gabe offered a slow, handsome smile, and his face and ears turned a bright red. He said nothing, returning his attention to his food.

Meredith dared to look around at their friends. Roxie and Perry winked at each other; Enid and Hugh smirked; Idella appeared perplexed; and Richard was too busy eating his mid-day meal to notice. This event would certainly be fodder for the gossip mill.

Finally, Roxie, bless her heart, brought up the subject of the weather.

## Chapter Seven

OVER THE PAST FEW years, the Waller and Kleeman families had spent a lot of time together. But that was when Gabe was in Missouri. With Gabe's return, visiting each other's families had become a trifle awkward.

As they walked toward Gabe's home the following Saturday evening, Meredith noticed that Mama and Mrs. Kleeman began chatting about the happenings around town and how Charles was assisting Widow Jones this evening. Behind them, Pa and Mr. Kleeman chatted about grain prices. In the back, Tillie and Lula giggled about schoolgirl notions. Soon Gabe fell into step with Meredith.

The silence between Meredith and Gabe was awkward, but not as awkward as Lula and Tillie's giggles and whispers. Meredith could only imagine what they must be saying and she was sure it involved her and Gabe, especially since news of the potluck incident had reached its way to Tillie's ears.

"Sure has been nice weather," Meredith commented, just to take her mind off of the discomfort she felt.

Gabe avoided her gaze and continued down the road. "Uh, yes, it has been."

"I wouldn't trade the summers in Ellis Creek for anything. Not that I've lived anywhere else, mind you, to know about the summer season in other places." Yes, she was rambling. Meredith closed her mouth and worked her lip between her teeth. Why must she always sound like a blabbering ninny? It didn't help that Gabe proved not to be the most proactive conversationalist.

What must he think of her? Meredith tried not to stare at his strong and handsome profile. Why had she not noticed what a dapper man he was before this year? Clearly, she had been spending far too much time sewing dresses and far too little time noticing the man she'd known since they were children in school.

"How were the summers in Missouri?" There she went again. Her mouth opened before she could tell it to remain closed.

"Uh...reckon they were fine. Humid."

Gabe kept his focus forward. Why was the man so difficult to talk to? Did he think her a simpleton?

"Are you glad to be back in the Montana Territory?"

More giggles and snorts from the obnoxious factory greeted Meredith's question to Gabe and she noticed that if Lula and Tillie were any closer, they would be stepping on her heels. She whirled around and narrowed her eyes at her sister.

"Yes."

"That's good."

"That's good," Tillie mimicked Meredith in an exaggerated voice.

It was then that Meredith noticed that the girls had been copying everything she and Gabe had said, with Tillie mimicking her and Lula mimicking Gabe. Meredith had every mind to let that little sister of hers know that if she didn't stop posthaste, Tillie would be doing all of Meredith's chores on top of her own until Tillie was at least fifty-six.

She again turned and glared at the girls.

Gabe caught her glare and a deep blush covered Meredith's face. Oh dear. Now he must think of her as harsh. Meredith faced forward once again. It was just far too difficult to carry on a conversation with Gabe, the man of few words, especially with two annoying pestilences mocking every bit of the nearly one-sided conversation.

They reached Gabe's ranch, and fortunately, Gabe joined his father in showing Meredith's pa the barn, the corrals, and finally, the humble home.

"Impressive for a man so young, wouldn't you agree, dear?" Mama asked.

Meredith didn't need to see Gabe's ranch to be impressed. She was already captivated by his love for the Lord, his kind and thoughtful ways, and, of course, his dapper appearance.

Yesterday, Roxie had asked Meredith if she fancied Gabe. Meredith admitted it, to which Roxie had exclaimed, "Wouldn't it just be wonderful if the two of you began to court?"

"He doesn't even know I exist," Meredith had answered.

"Oh, he knows you exist all right."

"How can you be so sure?"

"Trust me. He sees you, Meredith."

Meredith hadn't told Roxie about the secret letters she'd been receiving, although she had been tempted to share the news. It was one of those rare things she decided to keep even from her best friend.

If only the man who was delivering the letters could be someone like Gabe instead of the likely prospects of Leopold Arkwright, Marvin Pratt, or Mr. Griggs.

Thinking back on her conversation with Roxie, Meredith wished she could see the big picture the Lord saw, instead of the small tintype she managed. Then she would know for sure if Gabe fancied her, or at the very least, knew she existed.

Gabe tossed a pile of hay to the horses in the corral. If he showed wisdom in how he spent his earnings, he should be able to add a few more cattle to his herd by next year. If he continued to grow his herd, he should be able to provide a nice home for the woman he would someday marry.

Marriage?

Meredith Waller had messed with Gabe's mind. He had never even contemplated marriage until he'd returned from Missouri and seen Meredith sitting in church.

The woman he'd never truly forgotten.

What must she think of him? After the potluck and him thudding his head into hers while she reached for the handkerchief, she must think of him as a buffoon. A woman as lovely as her could have a choice of any man to court. Why would she choose someone like him? Someone who was clumsy and wordless?

Although, Gabe had to admit, his speaking when around her had improved, thanks to the countless prayers he'd sent heavenward. While they were walking to his home with the families last week, he had actually said more than one word at a time. Twice. He had actually articulated words, rather than grunts, in her presence. God was steadily helping him improve. Hopefully, those small improvements would be enough to win her heart.

Gabe perused the area around his ranch. With the exception of the animals, he was alone. Perhaps this would be as good a time as any to practice his speaking skills. He beckoned his horse, Dottie. She ambled toward him and he fed her an apple. "Now, Dottie, I need your help. You see, there's this girl named Meredith. I've fancied her for many years." Gabe paused and scanned from right to left, just to be sure no one had arrived at his ranch.

Seeing no one, he continued. "Dottie, I'm going to pretend you are Meredith, so I can work on my speaking skills. For some reason, I'm tongue-tied beyond belief when I'm in her presence. Are you ready?" As if she understood, Dottie nodded her head and neighed.

"Hello, Meredith. You look beautiful today. You have the prettiest blue eyes I've ever seen." Gabe grinned and tried his best to imagine Meredith stood before him, rather than his horse. "Reckon it is still two months away, but I would be much obliged if you would attend the—" he paused. He really had to practice this part so he wouldn't make the same mistake he'd made years ago when he'd called the barn dance a *yarn bance*.

"I was wondering if you'd accompany me to the harvest barn dance at the Randels'."

Dottie seemed distracted, as she nodded her head to and fro.

"Is that a yes?"

Giggles and snorts interrupted Gabe's conversation. He turned to see Lula snickering behind him. He felt his face flush as he gritted his teeth. When had she arrived and how much had she heard? "Lula, what are you doing here?"

"Watching you carry on a conversation with a horse." She started giggling again.

"Don't you talk to your pets at home? I reckon you've spoken to your puppy many times."

"True, but I never pretended he was Meredith!"

"Lula, you will not tell anyone about what you just saw."

"I won't?" With that, Lula took off down the road, her long braids flying behind her.

Gabe ran after her. He recalled a time, not too far in the past when he couldn't run to save his life. His weak legs could barely walk on some days. But not today. God had healed him, and he would catch that impudent sister of his if it was the last thing he did.

With his long stride, it didn't take long to catch up to her. "Lula, please stop."

Lula whirled around to face him, her face flushed from laughing so hard at his expense. "Will you please not tell anyone about what you saw and heard here today?"

She seemed to ponder his question. "So, you admit that you were pretending that Dottie was Meredith and that you were telling her how beautiful she is with her pretty blue eyes?"

Gabe sighed. "All right. I admit I was practicing my speech for Meredith on Dottie."

"That's what I thought. So, you do like Meredith then?"

"Maybe."

"For a bag of jawbreakers, I might be persuaded not to utter a word about this to anyone." Lula paused, then whispered, "except Tillie."

"For a bag of jawbreakers, you'll not utter a word to anyone, not even Tillie."

Lula's shoulders slumped. "But she's my best friend."

"Not even Tillie, Lula."

"All right. I'll do my best."

"Were you stopping by for a visit?"

"Ma wanted me to invite you to supper." Lula's eyes darted to and fro as if she were hiding something. Of all the sisters God could have given him, the good Lord had to give Gabe a mischievous one.

"Lula, you're acting mighty peculiar."

Lula shifted her shoes in the soft dirt. "I just might have an idea, that's all."

"An idea?"

"An idea to help you be able to speak to Meredith without being such a shy fellow."

So Lula had noticed. Just grand. "What's your idea?"

"Not so fast. First, you must agree to two things."

"Two things?"

"Yes. First, you must agree that I may call an important meeting with Tillie to discuss this matter before I share with you my magnificent idea."

Gabe exhaled. This was not boding well for him. "And second?"

"Second thing is that you, under no circumstances, can be angry with me for my idea or any ideas in the past."

"This sounds suspicious, Lula. Reckon I can't agree to your terms."

Lula folded her arms across her chest. "Then I'm afraid I can't tell you my idea, and you will really want to hear it."

"All right, all right," Gabe said, after offering prayers for patience. "I reluctantly agree to your terms."

"Then give me an hour and I'll be back to present my idea to you before supper." With that, Lula bounded off, braids flying behind her, as she headed toward their parents' home.

True to her word, Lula returned about an hour later. Gabe had agonized about her idea. It would either be an impressive one, or it would be the worst idea he'd ever heard. He banked on the latter.

"I spoke with Tillie. She regrets she is unable to attend this meeting due to the fact that she may have exaggerated about having her chores completed. Sometimes children make bad decisions of that sort."

Gabe narrowed his eyes at Lula. Hadn't she pulled that same antic with their parents a time or two?

"So Tillie and I did something. Now, remember, Gabe, you promised not to be angry about anything I am about to tell you."

"Go on, Lula."

"You see, some time ago, Tillie and I decided we wanted to become sisters forever. The only way to do that was for us to convince you and Meredith to get married."

"What?"

"Wait. It gets much better. We had this grandiose plan to write letters to Meredith from you."

"Write letters to Meredith from me?"

"Is there an echo on this ranch?"

Gabe shook his head. "Lula, please tell me you did not write letters to Meredith from me." If Meredith didn't already think him a buffoon, she certainly would after some crazy letters supposedly from him.

"We did. But here's the good news. We've only written..." Lula counted on her fingers. "We've only written her five of them."

"Five?"

"Yes. And more good news. We signed them from a 'secret admirer.' According to a good source, Meredith does not suspect it is you writing the letters."

A good source? That could only mean Tillie.

Whom did she suspect? It could be good...or bad that Meredith did not suspect him. Did she wish it was a certain fellow? Someone like Leopold Arkwright? Gabe had seen many an unmarried woman swooning over him a time or two. "I can't believe you and Tillie did that."

"Some call us geniuses. I prefer the term 'creative.'"

*More like impish.* "How can this help me?"

"Well, she has written back. Her letters are rather dull and full of questions, but if you started really writing the letters—" Lula paused for effect—"if you really were the one writing the letters, you could win her heart without even uttering a word."

Gabe mulled over Lula's words. This might not be so bad after all. Surely on paper, he could say things he would never have the nerve to say in person. "Reckon I could give it a try. How are you delivering the letters?"

"In the sliver in the knot of the old oak tree near the Jones' place."

"Do you have the letters she's written?"

"For a bag of jawbreakers for Tillie, she says I can give them to you."

Gabe would be poor for certain if he continued to spend his hard-earned money on jawbreakers. "This is bribery, Lula."

Lula shrugged. "I think Meredith would delight in receiving letters from you. You could ask her questions and find out more about her. Then when you fall in love you'll know what her favorite color is and all those good things to know about the woman you court."

The crazy idea could work. Perhaps through the letters, Gabe could gather the courage to make his intentions toward a particular young lady known.

If his letters to Meredith were deemed as favorable.

And if he could write better than he could speak.

## Chapter Eight

THE LETTERS ARRIVED WITH more regularity, but that wasn't the only thing Meredith noticed had changed. The handwriting had also changed. Her curiosity piqued. Had this suddenly become a prank? Were there two authors?

She would have to ponder this latest development.

Meredith shut the door to the room she shared with Tillie. She certainly did not want her younger sister to know about the letters. Tillie would undoubtedly share that tidbit of juicy gossip with Lula, who would manage to find a way to share it with others until the entire town of Ellis Creek was privy to the letters. Or they would find a way to publish it in the *Ellis Creek Journal*, which was always on the lookout for intriguing stories. Meredith cringed at that thought.

She plopped on the bed and noticed an open bag of jawbreakers on the chest of drawers she and Tillie shared. It certainly seemed as though Tillie ate far more jawbreakers than usual as of late.

Brushing the strange observation aside, Meredith opened her stash of letters and dumped them on the quilt to peruse. There had been five letters in the same handwriting and now two more recent letters in different handwriting, so seven letters total. She didn't recognize the penmanship of either batch of letters, but the second batch appeared more deliberate, interesting, and thorough.

She reached for a piece of stationery and penned a letter. Since her admirer hadn't been clear about his residence in one of his past letters, she decided to again address the issue. Knowing if he resided here would certainly assist her in determining his identity:

*Dear Secret Admirer,*
*Are you a man of religion? For what are you most grateful? Do you reside in Ellis Creek?*
*Yours Truly,*
*Meredith Waller*

The response arrived in two days.

*Dear Miss Waller,*

*Yes, I reside in Ellis Creek. Yes, I am a man of religion and a devoted follower of Christ. I am most grateful for the many blessings He has given me, including family and good health. For what are you most grateful?*

*Yours Truly,*
*Your Secret Admirer*

Meredith read and re-read the most recent letter. While thankful that he loved the Lord and had gratitude, she was determined more than ever to solve the mystery.

Stopping at the mercantile the following day, Meredith spied Marvin Pratt. Could he be the one who was writing to her?

She hoped not.

Although, he would be better than the other possible admirers. Meredith stood next to the shelf containing the sugar and flour and attempted to spy on Mr. Pratt while remaining discreet.

Marvin Pratt held a list in his hand and handed it to Mrs. Burris, the proprietor. "I'll be needin' these items for my Ma."

"Very well, Marvin. Give me just a moment."

Mrs. Burris, who with her severe hair and glasses, reminded Meredith more of a schoolmarm than a co-owner of the lone mercantile in Ellis Creek, bustled about locating items for Mr. Pratt. When she finished, she placed the list on the counter and began calculating the total due.

"That'll be three dollars and eighty-seven cents," she told her customer.

Mr. Pratt dug his hands into his trouser pockets. "Can you put that on my Pa's account?"

"Certainly."

"Thank you." Mr. Pratt grabbed the crate with some effort and seemed to rest it on his protruding stomach for ease of carrying it. "Well, hello there, Miss Waller. Pleasure seeing you here today."

"Hello, Mr. Pratt."

"What brings you out on this fine day?"

"Oh, just some errands. And you?"

"Retrieving some items for Ma. She's making my favorite supper tonight: meatloaf with mixed vegetables. Couldn't survive one day without her fine cookin.'" Mr. Pratt paused. "Reckon I enjoyed the church sermon a whole lot this past Sunday. Am thankful that my back isn't giving me grief like it does on occasion."

Meredith swallowed hard. Hadn't her secret admirer mentioned he was a man of God and thankful for good health?

Not that Marvin Pratt wasn't a nice man. On the contrary, he had always been polite. But at age thirty, he hadn't yet found a way to live on his own without the care of his parents. "Have a fine day, Mr. Pratt."

"You as well, Miss Waller." With an amiable bob of his round head, Marvin Pratt exited the mercantile.

And that's when Meredith saw it. Mr. Pratt's item list. Could it be the key to solving the letter mystery?

She hoped the list was in Mr. Pratt's penmanship, rather than his mother's.

"Mrs. Burris, may I see that list?"

Mrs. Burris gave Meredith a befuddled look. "Mr. Pratt's list of items?"

"Yes, ma'am."

With a perplexed facial expression, Mrs. Burris handed Meredith the list. It was a man's penmanship, Meredith was sure about that. But it didn't match the handwriting of either batch of letters she had received.

She let out an enormous sigh. "Thank you, Mrs. Burris." Eyeballing her own list, she added, "I see that I need some baking powder."

Mrs. Burris's eyes rolled behind large wire-rimmed spectacles. "Oh, that's why you needed to see Mr. Pratt's list. So you could discern what item you had forgotten. I thought as much."

Meredith didn't want to lie, so she instead smiled. She offered a prayer of gratitude that Marvin Pratt was one more person to mark off her list of possible suspects.

Gabe found that he enjoyed receiving and writing the letters. But most of all, receiving them. Meredith had elegant penmanship and each letter held her soft scent of lavender. Who'd have thought he, Gabe Kleeman, man of few words, would become the author of letters? And who would have thought that Lula and Tillie would have actually thought up a worthwhile idea?

Of course, the letters the two best friends had written made Gabe cringe. Especially the poem. He would never write anything like that. Ever. Gabe did not consider himself a poet in any sense of the word and he had never been syrupy or lovey-dovey.

Through the letters, he found that he and Meredith had much in common. Not that he had ever doubted that. Having known her since school, he knew they shared many similar interests.

Gabe read her most recent letter:

*Dear Secret Admirer,*
*What traits do you most admire in others? What things in life vex you most?*
*Yours Truly,*
*Meredith Waller*

The answers to those questions weren't difficult, although Gabe was glad he was writing the answers, rather than speaking them. Tillie had offered him stationery, and in his best penmanship, he wrote:

*Dear Miss Waller,*
*The traits I most admire most in others are kindness and helping those in need. What traits do you admire most in*

*others? The things that vex me most are liars, those riding through town too quickly and nearly running someone over. What most vexes you?*

*What is your favorite color?*
*Yours Truly,*
*Your Secret Admirer*

Gabe placed the letter in his trouser pocket. Later today, he would ride into town and deliver it. While it was costly to keep Lula and Tillie in jawbreakers, it had been worth it. Gabe had all of the letters they collected from Meredith. He also had their promised silence.

What would become of this odd situation? Would Meredith ever find out it was him who had written the letters—well, the most recent letters? If she did find out, would she be thrilled or disappointed? Perhaps she'd rather it be someone like the wealthy Leopold Arkwright.

Two days later, Gabe found a letter from Meredith in the tree. The objective was to avoid being there when Meredith was, lest she discover his secret. So far, he'd been lucky in that aspect. Climbing on his horse, he rode a short stretch before opening the letter:

*Dear Secret Admirer,*

*Thank you for your letter. I am glad you appreciate helping those less fortunate. I, too, agree that liars and those riding too quickly through town are vexing. For me, I would add that sewing a crooked seam and having to re-sew it is irritating as well. Another thing that perturbs me is ungentlemanly behavior. As for traits I admire most in others, those would include honesty, thoughtfulness, and loyalty.*

*My favorite color is purple.*
*Yours Truly,*
*Meredith Waller*

Gabe caught the scent of Meredith's perfume on the letter and inhaled. He had been giving the letters much thought lately. Perhaps it was time to reveal who he was to her. But then again, maybe not. What if Meredith abhorred the thought of him being her secret admirer? While she was pleasant whenever they met in person, Gabe figured she likely had several other suitors vying for her hand in courtship.

One of them was likely that brash Leopold Arkwright. Would Gabe have a chance against someone as wealthy and dapper as Leopold?

If Meredith discovered it was Gabe who sent the letters, would she be thrilled? Or would she kindly reject him? Forget about when he told her. How would he tell her? While the Lord had given him assistance in the shyness department, Gabe still struggled with stringing words together in her presence.

Gabe nudged Dottie into a gallop as he passed by the Randels' farm. That's when an idea came to him.

Later that evening, he penned yet another letter to Meredith:

*Dear Miss Waller,*

*Are you attending the barn dance at the Randels' next week? I plan to attend and would like very much the honor of dancing with you. I will be wearing a red bandana on my left arm.*

*Yours Truly,*
*Your Secret Admirer*

## Chapter Nine

MORE LETTERS HAD ARRIVED in recent days, and Meredith again contemplated the conundrum of why the most recent letters contained different handwriting than the earlier ones. If she were a Pinkerton detective, she would have already solved this mystery.

As she shoved open the door to the Ellis Creek National Bank, an idea came to her. Perhaps she could cross another likely letter-writer off her list by asking for a sample of Leopold Arkwright's penmanship.

"Well, Miss Waller. To what do I owe the pleasure?" Leopold Arkwright adjusted the glasses on his pointed nose and offered her a wide grin.

A grin that rendered many eligible women in Ellis Creek flustered and giddy. But not Meredith. Mr. Arkwright's "charms" had no effect on her.

Meredith retrieved her coin purse and placed four coins on the counter. "I'd like to make a deposit, please, Mr. Arkwright."

"Certainly." Mr. Arkwright leaned toward her through the banker's window and offered a coquettish wink. "How are you this fine day, Miss Waller?"

Meredith took in the site of Leopold Arkwright's mutton chop whiskers, which framed his narrow aristocratic face; his thick glasses; and his even thicker eyebrows; and she offered a silent prayer heavenward: *Lord, please, can my secret admirer not be Leopold Arkwright?*

Not that the man wasn't amicable, because he was. However, Mr. Arkwright had an excessive sense of self and his intentions were a bit forward. "I'm fine, Mr. Arkwright. And you?"

"Doing quite well. I certainly appreciate you choosing to do your banking at Ellis Creek National Bank."

Meredith didn't mention that the Ellis Creek National Bank was the only bank in town.

She pushed aside her thoughts of banking and deliberated about the real reason she had visited the bank: to discover if Mr. Arkwright was her secret admirer. Had he written any or all of the letters to her? She pushed aside the dismal thought.

"Mr. Arkwright?"

"Yes, Miss Waller?"

"Could I kindly ask a favor of you?"

"Most certainly. A buggy ride? A picnic? Accompaniment to the Randels' barn dance next week?"

At the latter, Meredith widened her eyes, and her heart raced. Hadn't one of the most recent letters mentioned the Randels' Barn Dance?

"No, no thank you, Mr. Arkwright. Rather, could you please write *dearest bandana dance* on a slip of paper?"

"Dearest bandana dance? Why, Miss Waller, you are not only winsome, but you also have a marvelous sense of humor." Leopold Arkwright threw his head back with a chortle, causing his neatly combed hair to flutter to the other side of his head.

Without hesitation, the banker retrieved a slip of paper from his desk and wrote the words Meredith had requested. She held her breath. He then pushed it through the teller window toward her. "Now then, is that what you requested?"

Meredith glanced at the writing, but she couldn't ascertain if it was the same writing as the writing in the letters she had received. Did all men write in a similar fashion? "Could you please write the words...?" Meredith made a show of pretending to think up more silly words. "Could you also write the words *secret, forward,* and *barn*?"

"At your service, dear lady."

Meredith did her best not to roll her eyes at the banker's exaggerated words and posture. He wrote the words on the same piece of paper, then again slipped it under the teller window. "Thank you, Mr. Arkwright."

"My pleasure. Now tell me, Miss Waller, shall I convene with your father and request his permission to accompany you to the annual barn dance at the Randels'?" His thick dark bushy eyebrows knitted together to form one long substantial eyebrow.

*Such a presumptuous man!* "My apologies, but I will have to decline. Perhaps another time."

"Not to worry. As they say, it is to man's benefit to be patient, as long as he is waiting on such a handsome woman as yourself. Although, I must say, I have been secretly admiring your loveliness."

Meredith swallowed hard. Had he just said secretly admiring? Did that mean secretly admiring by letter? She suddenly felt faint.

"If you'll excuse me." She grasped her coin purse, the slip of paper with his writing sample on it, then with what was left of her dignity, she hurried out of the bank.

Never, ever had she ever wanted anything so badly as to not be the object of Mr. Arkwright's affections or his letters. While some women in Ellis Creek would be honored to capture the man's fancy, Meredith was decidedly not one of them.

Later that afternoon, Meredith sat under the large cottonwood tree at her parents' home. The letters she had received lay sprawled before her, open. Beside the letters, she had placed Leopold Arkwright's penmanship sample.

Counting on her fingers, she listed the things she knew to be fact. She knew that her secret admirer resided in Ellis Creek. At church last Sunday, she had glanced around several times to see if she could spot any other young unmarried men she'd not known of before.

Her eyes had lingered on a certain Gabe Kleeman. Unfortunate that he couldn't be the author.

Meredith knew the first letters were written in different script than the latter letters. Could it mean two different admirers? If so, that led to a larger conundrum.

Reaching for her pencil, Meredith jotted down the names of her possible admirers with notes beside each name.

*Marvin Pratt: Handwriting does not match; however, discussed topics that could be related to topics mentioned in previous letters.*

*Mr. Norman: Never really a suspect. Old enough to be my great-grandfather.*

*Mr. Griggs: Lack of teeth, failure to bathe, never has expressed interest.*

*Leopold Arkwright: Handwriting may or may not match (difficult to ascertain); could be a possibility; asked about dance in person.*

*Gabe Kleeman: Wishful thinking. Does not even know I exist.*

Meredith bit the inside of her lip. Was there anyone she was missing? If not, then all clues pointed to Leopold Arkwright. If that was the case, she would cease writing to him immediately, and she for certain would not look for him at the barn dance.

Tillie took a sip of her lemonade. She loved attending the barn dances with Lula. Once in a while, someone even asked Tillie to dance, but mostly it was that vexatious boy named Willard, who sat in front of her in school. His flaming, bright red hair gave Tillie a warning anytime he was about to approach her. "Have you seen Willard?" she asked Lula.

"Not yet. I'm sure he'll be here to ask his favorite girl for a dance." Lula winked and giggled.

"Meredith says that boys don't always stay peculiar as they get older. If Willard wasn't so downright idiosyncratic, I might take a liking to him. Do you think there's any hope for Willard?"

"No. Boys are all odd if you ask me. Say, what do you think Meredith thought of the latest letters? Do you think she realizes the writing is different?"

Tillie shrugged and popped a jawbreaker in her mouth. "If she has any suspicions, she hasn't mentioned them to me. I'm just glad Gabe knows about the whole situation now. Makes things a lot easier with him writing the letters."

"Meredith does look a bit sheepish over there by the punch bowl. Do you suppose she's waiting to see who walks in with a red bandana?"

"Won't she be surprised! I don't think she has any clue it's Gabe. I know that Mr. Arkwright down at the bank fancies her. Say, there he is right now." Tillie pointed toward the entrance.

"We for sure cannot have Meredith marrying Mr. Arkwright. How will we ever be sisters forever if that happens?"

Tillie looked at her friend's concerned face. "No, we mustn't allow Mr. Arkwright to set his sights on Meredith. It's a right good thing Gabe is smitten with her too." Tillie watched as Mr. Arkwright approached her sister. "A right good thing indeed."

## Chapter Ten

MEREDITH ATTEMPTED NOT TO appear nervous, but she knew she wasn't successful. The man who'd written her the letters would be arriving any moment, if he wasn't here already.

She eyed the many people in attendance. Her parents were already dancing, as were Mr. and Mrs. Kleeman. Roxie and Perry were sipping lemonade on the sidelines, and Tillie and Lula stood in a nearby corner whispering and sharing giggles. Where was Gabe Kleeman? Had he decided not to come with the rest of his family? Meredith felt a twinge of disappointment in her heart. Would Gabe ever know of her secret admiration for him? Would he ever feel the same for her? The man rarely spoke and seemed to not even notice her presence. Had someone else captured his fancy?

"Care to dance?" Marvin Pratt sidled up alongside her with a hopeful grin on his pudgy face.

"I'll have to pass at the moment, Mr. Pratt, although I appreciate your inquiry."

Marvin hung his head and pooched out his bottom lip. "All right, Miss Waller. But if'n you wanna dance, I'll be happy to oblige."

Meredith acknowledged his response politely, grateful there was no bandana on Mr. Pratt's beefy arm. Ma would have her hide and then some if she wasn't anything but polite. But she didn't want to dance with Mr. Pratt. No, she wanted to wait and see who the man was who'd been writing her the letters—the man who had promised to attend the barn dance with a red bandana around his arm.

She squinted toward the entrance just as Leopold Arkwright sauntered in, his arrogance emanating across the room.

Meredith gasped. His red and black shirt caught her attention. She squinted in an attempt to reassure herself that a red bandana had not blended in with the pattern. His gaze connected with hers and he strutted toward her. Was there still time to hide?

"Fancy seeing you here, Miss Waller." Leopold Arkwright coyly grinned at her, exposing a mouth full of far too many perfectly straight teeth.

"Hello, Mr. Arkwright."

"From your comment at the bank the other day, I took it to mean you weren't going to be in attendance."

Meredith swallowed. To lie would never do. But how could she explain to the man that she hadn't wanted to attend with him in a proper and kind way? Coming to the conclusion there was no honest way, Meredith attempted a polite smile and avoided the question.

"Would you like for me to continue writing letters to you?"

Meredith's palms grew clammy and she tried her best to wipe them on her dress in as ladylike a fashion as possible. More letters? Had he been the one? "What letters?"

"Why, such as the letters you had me write in the bank the other day."

*He thinks those were letters?* Relief flooded over her. "Oh, those letters. No thank you, Mr. Arkwright. Now if you'll excuse me, I must—"

"Dance with me?"

Meredith didn't try to hide her shock at the man's cheeky behavior. "Not at the moment, Mr. Arkwright. Now if you'll please excuse me."

Hurrying past Leopold Arkwright, Meredith continued along the outskirts of the dance floor. She turned to take a second glance just to be sure Leopold wasn't following her.

That's when something most embarrassing happened. She ran right into Gabe Kleeman.

Gabe's arms reached for Meredith as she teetered toward him. When he righted her, Meredith's gaze connected with his. Gabe swallowed hard. Hadn't he often dreamed of holding Meredith in his arms?

Perhaps so, but not due to this awkward circumstance. "Hello...uh...Meredith," he said, hearing in his own ears that his voice sounded like the croak of an ill frog. He shoved the insecure thoughts aside. She smelled of roses and he inhaled again.

His heart leapt a bit in his chest just at the mere sight of her.

"Hello, Gabe."

Gabe realized he was still holding her in his arms, but to Meredith's credit, she didn't seem like she was trying her best to escape his gentle hold. He released her and took a step back and willed his mouth to speak rational and intelligible words. "Um...are you all right?" Not quite as intelligent-sounding as he'd hoped, but it would have to do.

Meredith nodded and pressed her hands against the wrinkles of her blue dress. My, but wasn't she a sight to behold! Realizing he was staring, Gabe averted his gaze toward the folks on the makeshift dance floor, then back again to Meredith. That's when he realized Meredith was staring at the red bandana on his arm.

What would she think now that she knew he was her secret admirer? Well, not her secret admirer exactly, as he'd just only recently begun to take over the task of writing letters to her. But still, would she be happy to discover his feelings toward her? Or disappointed? A wave of insecurity washed over him.

Meredith's gaze returned to his face, her expression unreadable. Should he ask her if she would like to dance? Prefer some lemonade? Escape his presence? The loud music sounded in Gabe's ears. "Uh..."

"Yes?"

Gabe took a deep breath. *Lord, please can You make my mouth work with coherent words?* "Uh...hello, Meredith." *It was a start, if not redundant.*

"Hello, Gabe."

What a fool he was! They'd already made introductions. "Meredith?"

"Yes?"

Was that expectation he saw in her eyes? He hoped so. She hadn't fled yet. That comforted him.

"Would you...would you care to step outside for a minute of fresh air?"

"Certainly."

Just speaking those fourteen words drained him of energy. But how else could he explain about the letters with all the commotion that surrounded them?

Gabe followed Meredith outside. Several other folks had the same inclination, as many couples and children were enjoying the fresh air. Gabe offered a prayer. He would need a miracle if he was going to be able to utter more than a few words.

Meredith's heart seemed as though it might just beat plumb out of her chest. Was Gabe sporting a handkerchief around his arm in case he needed to use it, or was he *the one*?

Her mind brimmed full with the memorized contents of all the letters she had received. If the handkerchief was on Gabe's arm because he was the one who had written them, it could only mean one thing.

He liked her as much as she liked him.

Would it be proper to ask him if he'd sent the letters? Just to be sure? Or should she wait for him to say the first word? What if he never said anything?

Meredith stopped by the fence post and watched a colt with boundless energy kick up its heels.

"I...uh...it's a nice night." Gabe had stopped beside her near the fence and wiped his hands on his pants. He looked quite dapper this evening with his blue chambray shirt that further enhanced his broad shoulders. He smelled of pine, like the forests near Ellis Creek. "It is a nice night."

They stood in silence for what felt like an hour. Gabe's ears had begun to turn red, a trait Meredith found endearing. She looked out over the sun that was starting to set. "Are you...are you the one who sent me the letters?" What would Mama say of her forwardness?

He took so long to answer that Meredith regretted asking the question. Perhaps Mama and Pa would announce it was time to return home and save her from this embarrassment. If Gabe said, "no," then what would he think of her? Yet, why did he sport the red handkerchief on his left arm? She leaned over just to be sure it was still there.

"Oh, there you are, Meredith." Tillie skipped toward her. "I was looking for you. Hello, Gabe."

That girl had the worst timing ever. "Did you need something, Tillie?"

"No. I was just wondering where you went. That impertinent Mr. Arkwright is looking for you."

Meredith grimaced. Would the man never realize she wasn't the least bit interested in him? "I'll thank you kindly not to tell Mr. Arkwright where I am." Meredith tossed a threatening big-sister-glare Tillie's way.

Tillie made a motion to appear she was buttoning up her lips. "Not a chance. I'd never do something cheeky like that. Mr. Arkwright is a cad if I ever knew one. But

Gabe here, well he's the opposite of a cad. A gentleman, to be precise."

"Thanks, Tillie." Good. Gabe had found his voice again. Now if Tillie would leave them to their discussion, Meredith might find the answer to her important question before nightfall.

"I better return to the dance. That ridiculous boy, Willard, with the pumpkin hair, persists in asking me for a dance."

Meredith laughed at her sister's exaggerated words. "Give him one dance, Tillie, and then rest assured he'll likely cease pestering you."

"That would be seemly, but highly improbable." Tillie rolled her eyes. "I'll leave you to your conversation."

"Thank you, Tillie." Meredith marveled at how intelligent her sister always sounded with her large vocabulary. The girl's dream of someday teaching school seemed attainable. With a swish of her skirts, Tillie turned on her heel and returned to the barn.

Would it be too brazen for Meredith to ask Gabe her question again? She chewed on her bottom lip. If she did ask again, might she receive an answer this time? If she didn't ask again and he hadn't heard her the first time, she might never know.

She must know.

Therefore, she must ask.

"Gabe, are you the one who wrote the letters to me?"

"Somewhat."

"Begging your pardon?"

Gabe cleared his throat. "I am somewhat responsible for the letters."

"Somewhat?" This conversation was going nowhere. Did he have a partner in writing the letters? Had he, or had he not, written the letters?

Gabe turned to face her. His eyes were so hazel. His handsome face so serious. Could it be she'd made some mistake? She hoped not. "Begging your pardon, Gabe, but I received a letter stating that the author would be wearing a red handkerchief on his arm at the dance. Have I mistaken the red one on your arm?" She hated the way her voice sounded so desperate. More than anything else at the moment, she truly wanted her secret admirer to be Gabe. What a wonder it would be if he had admired her from afar, just as she had admired him.

"I wrote the last five letters."

"Only the last five?" Then who had written the prior letters? *Please not Leopold Arkwright.* "May I inquire as to who wrote the previous letters?"

The corners of Gabe's mouth turned up in a large smile. He seemed to be able to converse easier now than in the past. "Our dear sisters."

"Tillie and Lula?"

"Two and the same."

Meredith put her hand to her chest. Her sister, along with Gabe's sister, had dreamed up this scheme?

"But then...how? Why?"

Gabe chuckled, a flush creeping across his handsome cheeks. He shrugged, but said nothing, so Meredith continued. "I suppose I don't rightly understand. Why would our sisters do something so unconventional? That would explain, however, why some of the letters were written in a different penmanship. I'm assuming that's because they wrote some of them and you wrote some of them."

Meredith paused to take a breath as she processed the information. "I'm surely thankful that your decision to wear a red handkerchief on your arm is because you are the one who sent the letters. Well, not all of the letters, mind you, but some of the letters. And I'm ecstatic that Leopold Arkwright didn't write any of those letters. After all, he mentioned writing letters, and I do declare, the thought of him being the one was enough to make a girl faint dead away from dread." She took a deep breath. "Oh, dear me. I'm rambling."

Meredith's oval face had taken on a rosy tint, one to match his own, to be sure. If she wanted to ramble, that was quite all right with him. He wouldn't even utter another word. Gabe would just watch Meredith's face light up with excitement as she spoke.

It was as if the words he wanted to say were mushed down in his throat and unable to make their way the short distance out his mouth. He tried to pretend she was someone else while explaining about Tillie and Lula, and it had worked for a second. But one look at her face, and he was reminded all over again that this was Meredith.

Meredith Waller.

The girl he had secretly admired and had looked upon with great fondness since their school days. While the words seemed to flow with more ease than ever before, there was no way the words would ever come easily in her presence. So just how was a tongue-tied oaf like himself supposed to ask her the important questions, like the question of courtship? Or how could he tell her how pretty she was or that he wished he'd written all the letters, not just the last few? With his luck, he'd probably drool all over the place from his tongue being tied in more knots than an unworkable rope. What then? Would she still be thankful that it was he, and not Leopold Arkwright behind the letters?

She was gazing at him expectantly, awaiting a response. He prayed, then mustered up some courage that must have come all the way from his curled toes in his boots. "Meredith." Her name caught in his throat.

"Yes?" Meredith's eyes were bright with anticipation.

"I…"

Her head bobbed slowly as she waited for him to speak.

"I…I'm glad it's me too."

"You're glad it's you?"

*Lord, could You please help me be long-winded just this once? I know You're in the business of miracles, and I reckon I could sure use one right about now.*

Gabe took a deep breath. "Meredith, I reckon I'm glad I'm your secret admirer and not Arkwright. I'm glad you're glad it's me and that I wore a handkerchief on my arm. I'm honored to be here with you tonight. I wanted to write all those letters, but I'm much obliged for our sisters starting off this whole thing." There. He'd said it.

And the Lord had performed a miracle.

An even brighter smile lit her face. "I can't wait to hear all about how Tillie and Lula ever came up with such a plan."

"Would you care to dance?"

"I'd love to dance."

Gabe led her back into the barn, relieved, for dancing was easier than conversation. He took her left hand in his and placed his right hand gently on her back. Every ounce of embarrassment had been worth it for this moment.

*Reckon you're turnin' soft, Kleeman,* he chastised himself.

Gabe drove Meredith home in his wagon that evening. She didn't want the night to end. Over and over, Meredith thanked the good Lord above that it hadn't been Mr. Arkwright or Marvin Pratt or Mr. Griggs who had been writing the letters.

She never would have guessed that Gabe fancied her.

The only sound during the ride home was the clop-clopping of the horses' hooves on the dirt road and the crickets in the night air. Meredith found the silence to be agreeable. It gave her time to rehash the night spent dancing with Gabe. Not once, not twice, but at least six dances. A time or two, she had noticed Leopold Arkwright starting to meander toward them, presumably to ask her for a dance. Gabe must have noticed too, for he quickly swept her aside.

Moments later, Gabe assisted Meredith from the wagon. "I had a nice time."

"Thank you, Gabe. I did too."

They stood facing each other. Meredith looked up into his eyes. His strong arms had been around her tonight, both when she'd run into him and then when they had danced. What would it be like to be kissed by Gabe Kleeman?

Meredith hastily chastised herself. A night spent in Gabe's company at a barn dance did not equal courtship. Although, she did hope he would ask to see her again.

## Chapter Eleven

WIDOW JONES PUT HER hand on Meredith's arm. "Thank you again for all the mending you've done for me."

Meredith smiled at the dear woman. "You are more than welcome, Widow Jones."

As they stood conversing, a wagon approached. The driver glimpsed their way, then took a second glance. He promptly turned the wagon around and headed toward Widow Jones's home. Meredith's heart stopped in her chest when she realized it was Gabe. She hadn't slept much last night thinking about their time at the dance and Gabe's admission to writing the letters. Maybe someday Meredith would even thank Tillie for her role in bringing them together.

And now, here the man of her affections was once again.

Gabe removed his hat. "Hello, Widow Jones." He turned toward Meredith. "I'd be much obliged if I could speak to you for a moment."

"Certainly. Is everything all right, Gabe?"

His face flushed before he answered a hearty "yes."

Widow Jones stood nearby, a smirk on her precious wrinkled face.

While waiting for him to continue, Meredith looked into Gabe's eyes. Such handsome eyes on such a handsome face. Not only that, but he was kind, generous, and a man of God. What was there not to like? How could she have not noticed him before he left for Missouri?

"Could you...would you...?" Gabe paused and threw a glance at the widow as if begging her to step aside. Was he hoping for a moment of privacy without their chaperone? What was he about to ask?

Meredith held her breath.

Gabe again darted his eyes toward Widow Jones in some type of unspoken message.

Instead of getting the hint, Widow Jones merely grinned, did the opposite, and took a step closer. To be privy to the interesting goings-on, perhaps?

"Meredith..."

"Yes?"

Gabe took a deep breath. "Would you do me the honor of courting me?"

"Yes, Gabe. I will court you."

Gabe nodded, returned his hat to his head, and strolled toward his wagon. With a wave, he beckoned his horses and rode off down the road.

Leaving Meredith to wonder if what had just happened was truly a reality.

Widow Jones held her hand to her heart. "Such a darling man. It befuddles me that he took so long to ask you. I could see it in his eyes the day you were both over here helping me that he fancied you. Ah, to be young and in love."

Meredith didn't have a response for Widow Jones, only that she was thrilled about what had transpired. Courtship with Gabe? She couldn't wait to tell Roxie.

"He does seem to suffer from a lack of words where you are concerned, dear," the widow continued. "Not to worry, however. My beloved Harold had a shyness about him as well until the day we married. Then he had words-a-plenty, and some mighty sweet words at that. Just takes some men a bit of time to find their words. Not one person who knew Harold would say he wasn't long-winded."

All this time, Meredith figured Gabe wasn't interested in her. But now, with their time spent at the barn dance, and his subsequent request for courtship, Meredith realized how wrong she'd been. Gabe had only been shy and reserved.

*Thank You, Lord. Thank You that You care about every detail in our lives. Even about courtship.*

Gabe's stomach knotted, as he rode his horse toward the Waller home. He had prayed since yesterday that he would summon the fortitude to do what he was about to do. If he survived this meeting, Gabe could survive anything.

Perspiration beaded his brow. What if Mr. Waller didn't find Gabe fit to court his daughter? What if Mr. Waller had someone else in mind for his eldest child? What if—

*Quit it, Gabe. You've given the situation to the Lord. It's only fitting you let Him handle it. Besides, if you can string enough words to ask Meredith today in front of Widow Jones, you can assuredly ask her father.*

*But then, once Meredith gave you her answer, you just rode off as hasty as a varmint escaping a predator. What must she think of that?* Gabe shook his head. He still needed assistance where shyness was concerned. A lot of assistance.

After scolding himself, Gabe experienced a renewed sense of courage. He traipsed toward the Waller home, noting that Tillie sat outside on the tree swing. "Hello, Tillie."

Tillie removed herself from the round circular chunk of log that constituted a swing. "Hello, Gabe. Say, I am about out of jawbreakers."

"Reckon you've had enough jawbreakers in the last few weeks to render you toothless."

"If you'd like me to keep your surreptitious messages to Meredith incognito, might I suggest another bag of jawbreakers?"

Gabe chuckled. "Nice try, Tillie. You forget I have a sister who has already attempted enough bribery in jawbreakers to last until she's forty-five. Anyhow, Meredith knows about the 'surreptitious messages' as you call them."

"She does?" Tillie's eyes grew large beneath her spectacles. "Who divulged the confidential information? The last I knew, she feared it was Leopold Arkwright delivering the letters."

"Meredith feared it was Arkwright?"

"She did. Or even that Mr. Pratt. Now, he's an interesting sort."

Gabe blew out a breath of relief. He needn't have worried that Meredith had wished the letters to arrive from Arkwright. Pratt had never been a concern. "So, do you think she's grateful it was me?"

"For a bag of jawbreakers—"

"No more jawbreakers, Tillie. Can you tell me where you pa is?"

"Reckon he's in the barn. What are you going to discuss with him?"

Gabe shook his head. The only downside of someday asking for Meredith's hand in marriage was that he would inherit another younger pesky sister.

Meredith was worth the sacrifice.

Moments later, Gabe found Mr. Waller in the barn. "What can I do for you, Gabe?"

"Hello, sir. May I have a moment of your time?"

Mr. Waller set aside his work. "What's on your mind?"

Gabe walked to the barn door and peeked outside. Sure enough, Tillie held her ear to the wall. He closed the door and returned to Mr. Waller. "I spied an eavesdropper."

Mr. Waller let out a rumbling chuckle. "That Tillie. God has some plans for her life for sure. But she's a bit on the meddlesome side."

Gabe couldn't agree more. But he hadn't come here to discuss Tillie's meddlesome ways. He removed his hat and reached his forearm up to wipe the perspiration on his forehead. "Mr. Waller, I've come to ask you an important question."

"Go on."

"I reckon I'd be much obliged if I could court your daughter." The words were out now and there was no retracting them. *Lord, please let him say yes.*

Mr. Waller narrowed his eyes, but said nothing in response. Gabe considered sneaking out of the barn, climbing on his horse, and returning home. Instead, he pleaded his case, drawing upon his rehearsed speech. "Sir, I have a right fine ranch that I'm continuing to expand. I will provide for Meredith and love her and care for her always."

"Just one question for you, son."

"Yes, sir?"

"What took you so long to ask?"

"Beg your pardon, Mr. Waller?"

"The Mrs. and I suspected that you've fancied Meredith for some time now."

Had everyone known of Gabe's intentions toward Meredith? "Yes, sir. Since we were in school together."

Mr. Waller raised his eyebrows. "We hadn't figured that long. Anyhow, you have my blessing to court my daughter. I couldn't ask for a finer man to make that request."

"You mean it, sir?"

"Yes, I do."

They shook hands until Gabe was certain he'd shake the hand right off the shorter, older man standing before him.

For two months, Meredith and Gabe had spent time together. Today, Gabe promised a picnic near the river, not far from Ellis Creek.

Meredith finished packing the picnic basket and then tucked in a checkered tablecloth she'd sewn last week.

"Are you departing with Gabe again?" Tillie asked, perching herself on the table.

"Yes. Today we're going on a picnic."

"That sounds romantic," Tillie swooned. "And to think, it all began with Lula and me and our brilliant idea."

"Thank you, Tillie."

"You're welcome. I received quite a few jawbreakers for our good deed." Tillie pushed her spectacles up on her nose. "Do you think someday Willard won't be such a nuisance? Maybe he'll be handsome and dashing like Gabe."

"That could very well happen, Tillie."

Tillie smirked and pointed out the window. "Here comes your beau now. I'll leave you to your swooning," she tittered, fleeing the room.

Less than an hour later, Gabe assisted Meredith from the wagon. She put her arm through the crook of his elbow as they walked toward the creek. Would God see fit to join them in matrimony someday?

Over the past couple of weeks, Gabe had improved in his shyness. Meredith giggled to herself. Perhaps what Widow Jones had said was true about men becoming more long-winded as time passed.

They looked into each other's eyes for a few moments until Gabe leaned toward her. "Meredith?"

"Yes?"

"May I steal a kiss?"

She thought he'd never ask. "Yes, you may."

He held her face gently in his large hands and leaned toward her. He smelled of pine trees and soap. She closed her eyes as his face neared hers. His mouth sought hers, the soft touch of his lips growing more passionate as the seconds passed. So this was what kissing Gabe would be like.

No disappointment there.

When the kiss ended, Gabe stroked her cheek with his finger. He seemed to be searching for words. "Meredith?"

"Yes?"

"Reckon I'm in love with you."

She reckoned—no she knew—that she was in love with him too. Meredith marveled how the Lord brought the right one to her in His timing.

Gabe suggested Meredith retrieve one final letter from the oak tree. He stood a short distance from her and watched as she reached her hand into the sliver for his letter. No more would he love the woman of his affections from afar.

Her dainty hands unfolded the note—hands he'd have the privilege of holding far into the future as they took long walks along his ranch. Their ranch.

Last week, Gabe had penned the words, *Will you marry me?* on some special lilac-colored stationery he purchased from the mercantile. Finally working up the nerve to deliver his letter, he held his breath for Meredith's response.

Her eyes scanned the paper, then gazed up at his. "Yes, Gabe. I will marry you."

In a romantic sweep, he had her in his arms. In an even quicker movement, his lips found hers, sealing the promise of their hearts.

# READ A SNEAK PEEK FROM
# *Love* UNFORESEEN

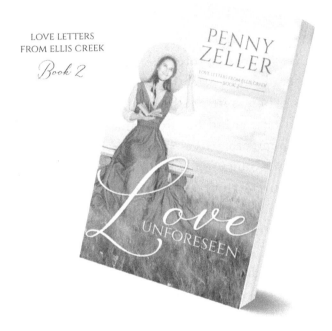

## WILL A BEST FRIEND'S MATCHMAKING SCHEME BE SUCCESSFUL?

# Love Unforeseen
## A Sneak Peek

Truth be told, her plan was most extraordinary.

Tillie Waller wrote the instructions on the chalkboard with perfectly large looping and slanted letters. Then, setting the chalk on the ledge, she took a seat behind her desk and anxiously waited for her pupils to arrive. She found her life's purpose in molding young minds at Ellis Creek School. Each day, she tirelessly thought of new ways to teach her students and encourage them to develop a lifelong love for learning.

Her pupils ranged in age from six to fourteen, and Tillie reminded herself not everyone would be able to complete the assignment without aid. No matter. She was always available to assist, and she had organized a group of older students who eagerly participated in helping the youngers.

"I have been in touch with my dear friend, Miss Amsel, in Fentonville. She is a teacher at the school there, and we both decided, posthaste, to treat our pupils to an extra-special assignment."

Tillie did her best not to giggle at the thrilled expressions on her scholars' faces. It was difficult for her not to become overly demonstrative in her presentation. "We will become pen pals with Miss Amsel's class. A benevolent Ellis Creek donor, who wishes to remain anonymous, has generously purchased enough postage stamps for us to mail many a letter to our new friends."

Respectful murmurs filled the room, and Tillie observed the same excitement from her pupils as she herself felt regarding this assignment. It would encourage writing and communication skills, as well as art skills. "I have written our directions on the chalkboard. We'll each write a letter and, if you'd like, you may also draw a picture to accompany your letter. Miss Amsel will dole out the letters to her pupils based on ages. Older children will receive an older child's letter, and so on. Those students will return letters to you with your names on them. Won't it be delightful to look forward to corresponding with our new friends?"

Faces lit with anticipation. It would surely seem a lifetime before Mr. Norman, the elderly postmaster, received the return letters from Fentonville and distributed them to Tillie's class.

Theodora, her friend, Lula's, six-year-old daughter raised her hand.

"Yes, Theodora?"

"Ooh, you mean we will be arthurs?"

"Authors, yes. Authors of letters. It will be quite thrilling." She passed out paper to each student.

The responses from their new pen pals couldn't arrive soon enough.

Will Fairbanks left Mr. Desmond's office, a new spring in his step. Finally, he would be back in Ellis Creek after all these years. As the new foreman for Desmond Mills, Will would oversee the mill operations.

And return to the town he missed.

A fleeting image of Tillie Waller, the girl he hadn't seen since his school days in Ellis Creek before his family moved to Fentonville, planted itself in his mind. Would she still be residing in Ellis Creek? Was she married? Would she recognize him?

He recalled her long auburn hair, soft green eyes, and overt appreciation for big words. That was one thing he always admired about Tillie: her intelligence.

Will had changed a lot in those eleven years since attending school in Ellis Creek. Had Tillie changed too?

Would she even notice his arrival? He'd pestered her enough to last a lifetime, and he doubted she missed him.

But he had missed her and thought about her from time to time.

Tomorrow, he would hitch up his wagon, load up his meager belongings, and take the day-and-a-half-long journey from Fentonville to Ellis Creek. He would visit the mill for the first time and secure a place to live. His nerves were on edge at the thought of supervising the crew at Desmond Mills in Ellis Creek. Ma, Pa, and Mr. Desmond all had confidence in him. The problem was Will wasn't sure he shared that confidence.

Praying yet again for wisdom and guidance, Will packed his bag and set it by the door. If he planned to leave before sunrise, he'd best get some shuteye.

If you want to be among the first to hear about the next release, sign up for Penny's newsletter her website at www.pennyzellercom. You will receive book and writing updates, encouragement, notification of current giveaways, occasional freebies, and special offers. Plus, you'll receive *An Unexpected Arrival*, a Wyoming Sunrise novelette, for free.

If you enjoyed this glimpse into the lives of Meredith and Gabe, please consider leaving a review on your social media and favorite retailer sites. Reviews are critical to authors, and those stars you give us are such an encouragement.

# Read a sneak peek from
# Forgotten Memories

SOME MEMORIES ARE BEST FORGOTTEN...

# Forgotten Memories
## A Sneak Peek

A FLEETING MOVEMENT CAUGHT twelve-year-old Annie Ledbetter's attention. She squinted at the grove of trees on a distant hill and willed her eyes to focus. A quick flash of something—or someone—appeared. Annie tipped her head to the left and stood on tiptoe, anticipating a better view.

The vacant prairie previously held nothing but miles and miles of grasslands, sagebrush, and the occasional rolling hill.

Until now.

Annie's feet stalled in the soft dirt as if rooted. Could it be? A man, or maybe more than one man, watched and scrutinized Annie and the rest of the travelers.

But as quickly as the figure appeared, he vanished.

A shiver of fear traveled up her spine.

Annie's heart skipped a beat and her arms tingled with numbness. What had she just seen? She rubbed her eyes and took a second glance, but now saw nothing. Stumbling, she began to walk again.

Should she mention what she had seen to Pa? Surely Pa, with his perceptive eyesight, had noticed the elusive movement. In the wagon, he and Ma carried on what appeared to be an important conversation, although Annie couldn't hear the words over the creaking of the wagon wheels and the commotion from the other families in their wagon train. Ma nodded at whatever Pa said, her hands propped comfortably on her large belly. The baby would be here soon.

Hopefully they made it to Nelsonville before that happened.

Annie stared in the direction of the grove of trees. Had she imagined what she'd seen? After all, Ma had commented on more than one occasion that Annie had an overabundance of imagination. If so, best not to tell Pa. He and her brother, Zeb, would give her a good ribbing about how the lonely boredom on the journey from their home in Hollins, Nebraska, to the Wyoming Territory, caused her to conjure up things that weren't really there. From the beginning of their trip several days ago, it had been an uneventful adventure with no Indian attacks, no severe illness among the travelers, and no unexpected deaths. Why should that change?

Annie rubbed her stomach then and groaned, attempting to appease the intermittent discomfort. Was it nervousness from what she thought she saw or were the berries she'd eaten at lunch causing a disturbance?

"Hiya, Annie." Zeb ran up alongside her and matched his steps with hers.

Annie diverted her attention from her nausea and turned to face her fourteen-year-old brother. She weighed her options. *Should I tell him about what I saw? Surely there would be no end to the teasing, but maybe he saw it too.*

"I think I saw someone hidden behind those trees."

Zeb shielded his eyes from the sun and focused where she pointed. "I don't see anyone."

"It must have been my imagination." Annie sighed and brushed aside a stray hair that had fallen from one of her braids. Zeb's confirmation somehow soothed her, yet her stomach was still in upheaval. "I wonder if we'll stop soon for supper."

To rest for a while sounded appealing.

"Our noonday meal wasn't that long ago. Are you all right?"

"I think the wild berries are causing a fuss in my stomach."

"Perhaps you can ride in the wagon for a spell."

Without awaiting her response, Zeb garnered Pa's attention, and moments later, Annie climbed into the back of the wagon, anxious to lie down in the hopes of settling her stomach.

The canvas provided a respite from the sun, even if the space was hot, crowded, and stuffy. The wagon housed all they owned and didn't leave much room for a growing twelve-year-old girl. Listless, Annie reached for her diary, the simple, well-worn book that had long ago become her companion. Perhaps penning an entry would relieve her nerves. She opened it and began to write for the first time since leaving her home.

*July 14, 1877*
*Dear Diary,*
*Pa says we will soon be reaching Nelsonville in the Wyoming Territory. I, for one, am thankful we are almost to our new home.*

*Having lost nearly everything and having to start over has been difficult for Ma and Pa, and I revisit often the memories of our old soddie and the mismatched round table and four chairs Grandpa Ledbetter gave Ma and Pa on their wedding day. I miss supper with stew, cornmeal muffins, and apple pie for dessert. Much more decadent than the plain beans we eat day after day on our journey.*

*Only one other family in our wagon train will settle in Nelsonville. Everyone else will continue to other destinations.*

*I had a nervous fright today when I thought I saw something in the distance, perhaps a man. I pray it was only my imagination.*

Caleb Ryerson stood beside his horse and watched as his older brother, Cain, peered through a brass monocular spyglass. Another plot to commit a crime. Would Cain and his friend, Roy, ever tire of taking things that didn't belong to them? Would they ever tire of ruining the lives of others?

Cain snickered. "You won't believe this, but that ain't no stagecoach that's comin'. It's a band of wagons."

He was crouched out of sight behind a grove of trees overlooking the valley where the travelers journeyed.

"What? I thought we was supposed to be watching for a stagecoach. Give me that." Roy Fuller grabbed the spyglass from Cain and peered through it. "Well I'll be. Little wagon train, likely four or five wagons."

Roy spit to the side, barely missing Cain's foot.

"Don't matter none, though. We can rob them just the same as we rob a stagecoach. And anyways, we might even get more loot out of the deal." Roy lifted the spyglass and gazed through it again. "Definitely ain't no big wagon train."

"I think we should stick to stagecoaches," Caleb interjected.

"Keep your opinions to yourself, Little Brother, 'cause no one even asked you," snapped Cain. "I'm tired of you trying to make 'polite' decisions. This ain't no time for politeness. As I've told you a dozen times, if you wanna eat, you'll do as I say. It's as simple as that."

Caleb sighed and kicked the soft dirt with the toe of his worn boot. He, Cain, and Roy had taken to robbing stagecoaches in a variety of Wyoming and Dakota Territory towns. Oftentimes, the loot was bountiful and the thievery simple. Twice there had been casualties. He cringed at the thought of his brother's and Roy's disregard for life and willed the memories to vanish from his mind. Those casualties had been someone's pa, brother, or son. He had never participated in taking the life of another and never would. His conscience wouldn't let him. If he someday wanted to leave the lifestyle he'd been born into, Caleb knew he would have to abstain from as much crime as possible, even if it meant suffering Cain's wrath.

"It pays better than trying to earn a living the honest way," Cain told Caleb on more than one occasion. "We're so good ain't no one ever gonna catch us. You'd think they'd have better lawmen in this part of the country."

Maybe the lawmen were smart and luck played a major role in their failure to be apprehended. What would happen someday when there was no more luck? Prison time? Hangings? Death from a gunfight like what happened to Pa? Caleb shivered. Would he ever escape the life he lived?

# Acknowledgments

To my family. Thank you for walking alongside me in this crazy writing life and for your patience while I live in my imaginary world.

To my readers. May God bless and guide you as you grow in your walk with Him.

And, most importantly, thank you to my Lord and Savior, Jesus Christ. It is my deepest desire to glorify You with my writing and help bring others to a knowledge of Your saving grace.

# About the Author

Penny Zeller is known for her heartfelt stories of faith and her passion to impact lives for Christ through fiction. While she has had a love for writing since childhood, she began her adult writing career penning articles for national and regional publications on a wide variety of topics. Today, Penny is the author of nearly two dozen books. She is also a homeschool mom and a fitness instructor.

When Penny is not dreaming up new characters, she enjoys spending time with her husband and two daughters, camping, hiking, canoeing, reading, running, cycling, gardening, and playing volleyball.

She is represented by Tamela Hancock Murray of the Steve Laube Agency and loves to hear from her readers at her website www.pennyzeller.com and her blog, *random thoughts from a day in the life of a wife, mom, and author*, at www.pennyzeller.wordpress.com.

Social Media Links:
https://linktr.ee/pennyzeller

## LOVE LETTERS FROM ELLIS CREEK

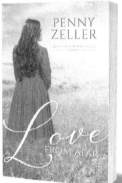

# WYOMING SUNRISE SERIES

# HORIZON SERIES

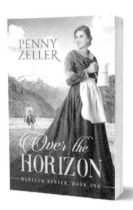

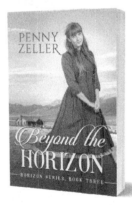

# HOLLOW CREEK

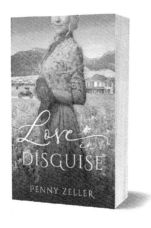

# STANDALONE BOOKS

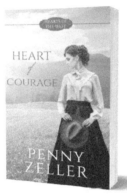

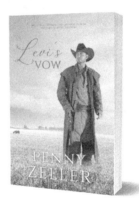

# CHRISTIAN CONTEMPORARY ROMANCE

## Love in the Headlines

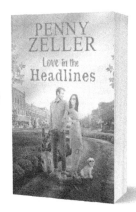

## Chokecherry Heights

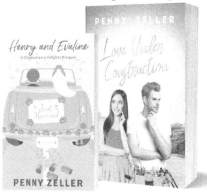

Made in the USA
Middletown, DE
26 April 2024

53413288R00081